# FROM
# ARTHUR'S
# SEAT

a collection of short prose and poetry

---

VOLUME 5 · 2020

FROM ARTHUR'S SEAT · VOLUME 5

From Arthur's Seat
University of Edinburgh
School of Literatures, Languages and Cultures
50 George Square
EH8 9LH

Published in 2020

Design and typesetting by Anna O'Connor
Cover images by Anna O'Connor

Typeset in Ten Oldstyle

Printed in the UK

ISBN: 978-1-8380121-2-0

ed.ac.uk
fromarthursseat.com

# FROM ARTHUR'S SEAT · VOLUME 5

## EDITOR'S NOTE

In my application to the Creative Writing MSc programme at the University of Edinburgh, I wrote that I was enthusiastic about *From Arthur's Seat* and hoped to make a meaningful contribution. The book you're holding just now is the result of a task that seemed at first, as do most tasks that are truly worthwhile, daunting as well as exciting.

In addition to being the anthology's editor-in-chief, I am also one of the authors. Many of the contributors were faced with a similar doubling of roles. This volume proves that we were equal to the challenge.

For many of us, this will be the first time our writing is published. This project was a great opportunity to learn what goes on behind the scenes, and what will be expected of us as writers. It is a true team effort, and a collection we are proud of. We hope you'll enjoy reading our work.

A note on the writing itself: this is an anthology produced by writers from all over the world, which is reflected in different varieties of English.

On the table of contents: we have included content warnings here, much like allergens on a restaurant menu, so that if there are topics you don't want to read about, we have hopefully provided you with a means to avoid them. For a comprehensive list of all sensitive material, please visit our website.

THANK YOU to everybody on the team. It has been a joy to work with you! On behalf of all of us, I would also like to thank our programme director, Jane McKie, and our writer in residence, Tracey S. Rosenberg, as well as all our tutors and professors on the Creative Writing MSc. Many of the pieces you're about to read were written during the programme, with guidance and advice from our teachers. THANK YOU. And lastly, to all the writers: now that we're going our separate ways, may we continue to push, help, and inspire each other, just like we did when we were making this anthology. THANK YOU. The 2019/20 academic year has certainly taught us how to communicate online, let's put that to good use.

This project has kept me busy in the best possible way during my year in Edinburgh. It has enhanced my experience to an extent I had not anticipated. It has proven to me yet again that when you have an opportunity, you should take it; especially if it's a challenge. You will learn and grow. Let's keep on taking those leaps!

This anthology is a celebration of our journey as writers, and of the community we have built while we were studying here in Edinburgh. We hope our joy in sharing the results with you shines through what you're about to read.

Lena Kraus
Editor-in-Chief

There are 52 students completing the Creative Writing MSc at the University of Edinburgh this year, a serendipitous figure. Too much can be read into numbers, of course, but there is something about the number 52 that is too good for any writer to ignore. 52 relates to *time*. There are 52 weeks in our calendar year. The period of a Mayan calendar – a Calendar Round – lasts 52 years.

This anthology represents a milestone in the development of these writers' lives and careers, where, over the course of the past year, they have been honing their craft – learning from their teachers, learning from each other, and, above all, learning to attend to their inner voices as they become increasingly proficient editors of their own work. We never seek to produce identikit writers on our programme: it is very much designed to support students in becoming the writers they want to be, and trying to equip them with the skills necessary to achieve that goal to the best of their ability. We hope this selection of stories exemplifies the range, diversity, and accomplishment of voices at Edinburgh this year. These stories and poems mark an important staging post on the continuing, thrilling journey these writers are embarking on.

The number 52 is associated with *play* as well. There are 52 white keys on a piano's keyboard. It is the number of cards in a standard pack of playing cards. Play implies adventure, a love of the journey as much as the destination. That sense of exploration is at the heart of the work in this anthology – sometimes playful, sometimes dark or daring, always immersive.

Finally, as Writer in Residence and Programme Director at the University of Edinburgh, we have the privilege of working with students from around the world. With a wide-ranging selection of themes, genres, and perspectives offered by an international group of writers, this year's volume of *From Arthur's Seat* offers a snapshot not simply of our MSc cohort, but of the times we live in, its challenges and worries and joys. As we write this, we are facing a pandemic, while political and ideological divisions continue to fracture countries and institutions. This anthology is a good way to remind ourselves of the ways in which individuals from around the globe can work and learn together harmoniously and creatively.

We have an exceptionally talented cohort of students on the MSc this year, for whom we have the utmost respect and admiration. We hope you enjoy reading their words as much as we do.

Tracey S. Rosenberg and Jane McKie
Writer in Residence and Programme Director

# CONTENTS

## POETRY

# POETRY

# PROSE

# PROSE

Content warnings: Sexual assault * Graphic content †
Suicide ‡ Miscarriage §

## TESS SIMPSON

*Last Summer*

They are late.

She hovers over the kitchen sink, slowly filling a glass of water. The heat is already shimmering over the road outside, warping the tarmac into ripples. Her dress – new, carefully chosen for the occasion – is sticking to her thighs and every few minutes she has to tug it down. The glass clinks against her teeth as she swallows. She's watching the road, listening for the roar of an engine.

She pulls her dress down.

There are little fruit flies hovering like a cloud around the softening fruit in the bowl, the stuff she had faithfully promised would be used – juiced, turned into a smoothie, whatever – and now a standoff has developed between her and her mother. They are each refusing to clean the rot away. She takes another sip of water, the glass sweaty in her hand. She looks out of the window again. Still nothing. She tugs her dress down. She moves towards the back door.

Her bag is ready, slouched against a pile of her brother's trainers, which permeate the room with a faint smell that's hard to pin down but impossible to ignore. She nudges it with her foot and it lolls open, revealing its contents. A crusty bottle of suntan lotion, some gummy lip gloss, a sandwich, condensation already beading its plastic wrapper.

Exams finished last week and she is giddy with freedom. This is that summer, the wild stretch of open space between one life and another. For two months she can turn herself into the person she wants to be, the person moving out of her parents' house in the autumn, the person with a life ahead of her full of parties and new friends and boyfriends and jobs and marriage and children and it all starts now, this summer, when she turns into the person she wants to be.

She tugs the dress down.

She had hoped that one of the things this new version of herself would be able to do is drive, but reality intervened when she failed her test a week ago. She now has to endure a long three-week wait until the next available test slot, so she is waiting for them, for her friends, who she is starting to suspect have progressed further down the path of self-improvement than she has.

She has started to worry. When they are all together in Maya's Ford Fiesta, screaming song lyrics into the twilight, it feels like they are already vanishing, already starting to remake themselves into people she can't reach. She has started to catch herself wondering who they are, these people she has spent the last six years of her life with. What does it mean that she thinks that they wouldn't like each other if they met for the first time now? Were they wrong about each other then, when they huddled together for protection in the scary first days of secondary school, moving in a tight pack around big echoing halls and deciphering the unspoken rules of this new environment? Or are they wrong now, so close to the end, with half a decade weighing them down? Do years alter souls the way they do faces?

She is sweating. This is unfortunate. The new dress is white and will show the stains. She holds her arms above her head, trying to cool down. The dress rides up. She tugs it down.

Her brother walks through the kitchen, bumping into her as he helps himself to some apple juice from the fridge, and she pulls a face at him behind his back. She doesn't have the energy for a fight right now, or rather she doesn't have the right kind of energy. It's all balled up in nervous anticipation in the pit of her stomach, rather than the loose anger she needs when she faces down her brother.

She loves him, and she thinks he still loves her, but she's not the only one trying on new identities. Home from university for the summer, he takes up more room than she remembers, laughs at jokes she doesn't understand and stays out late. They used to have film nights, bingeing though superhero films until dawn, getting into arguments about obscure comics lore and throwing popcorn at each other. He doesn't watch superhero films now. They are 'damaging the culture'. Instead, he has developed very strong opinions about Quentin Tarantino.

The energy has turned awkward with the two of them in the room and he's clearly not going anywhere, as he starts pulling out cheese and bread and pickles, so she drains her glass and puts it next to the sink, internally anticipating the world-weary sigh of her mother: 'The dishwasher is empty.' She leaves it on the counter and retreats into the sitting room, where she still has a view of the road. She pulls her dress down.

They are fifteen minutes late, which is not unusual. Maya and Rachel don't run by the same timetable as the rest of the world. They could be quite happy sitting in the middle of the school's playing field as the bell rang and the crowds disappeared, and it would be left to her to hurry them along, make sure they weren't late for the register, get them where they needed to be.

They would tease her for it.

'Yes, Mum, we're coming Mum.' They found it funny. She had laughed along because what else could she do, really? They were different from her, even then. Lighter, somehow. Freer. They seemed to know secrets about the world, like they had unlocked some cheat code about life that they just hadn't shared with her. Press X and R1 to learn how to talk to boys like a human being. Type 'skincare routine' in the dialogue box to learn how to apply foundation and cover up spots. Find the six hidden bonus coins to know how to drink alcohol.

Driving, that was one. She was a disaster every time she got behind the wheel, but they both passed first time. And now she is forced to rely on them for lifts, forced to wait until they deign to show up, always taking the corner way too fast, as if Maya has never been to her house before, skidding slightly as she adjusts, pulling to a too-abrupt stop outside.

And even when they are on the road, Maya is always distracted, glancing behind her, or checking her phone or skipping through songs to find her jam.

The sooner you pass your test, the better.

Maybe that will be the start of it, of the new life. Maybe the driving licence will mean that she is actually, finally, an adult. Maybe this is the thing that will make her feel the control that she expected, and never got from her first legal drink, or first time clubbing.

(They had pre-drinks at Maya's house before they went out, so Maya spent most of the night throwing up in the loos and Rachel started a fight with a girl who objected to Rachel making out with her boyfriend. That first time clubbing had ended with tears and a bloody nose and a contrite phone call home. Try feeling like an adult when you're picked up by your dad at one AM with two wasted friends and given a lecture about responsible attitudes towards alcohol the following morning.)

She adjusts the cushions on the sofa, smoothing and plumping them. She is ready to go, to get the day started, and they are still not here. They are going to the beach, and if they don't get there soon the car park will be full and all the good spots will be taken by tourists and families. They are going to spend the day there and take photos that will make their new university friends jealous when they scroll through them in a few months' time.

Look how relaxed and beautiful we are. Look how we know how to have a good time. Don't you wish you were with us?

Is that a car?

Close your eyes and you can see them, driving away from the house, taking the corner just a little too fast, speeding away towards something. A future, looming out of the distance in front of them, huge and unexpected and unknown. It is the summer when everything changes and who cares if they are going too fast to take in their surroundings. They are going to become different people this summer, now, maybe even this very evening. They are going to turn themselves into something completely new.

Look at us, she will think, as they speed away, three people on the verge of something, held together by a messy, fragile web of memories and history and habit.

Look at them. See them. Too late to warn them.

It's the summer when everything changes.

*Filet-O-Fish*

On my daughter's sixth birthday, she began to disgust me. It took me by surprise. For years I had taken care of her every need without hesitation. I had forced mashed carrots into her mouth, wiped shit from her asshole, picked out every bloody nit from her little head after her first grade class caught lice. But after that first wave of revulsion I could only wonder how it had not come to me sooner.

Lulu's birthday fell on a Thursday. Ben was out of town, on a trip for work. I liked to go out to eat when he was away—somewhere really trashy and convenient and delicious like McDonald's or the Chinese buffet. Ben had gotten obsessive about cholesterol recently. Several months ago, after a lifetime of heavy butter consumption, his father had suffered a heart attack while pulling his pants up—and now Ben was afraid to even piss sitting down.

I wanted a quarter pounder and fries, but Lulu was upset that her father wasn't home. Last year Ben and I had taken her to our favorite French restaurant downtown, the place we used to go for our anniversaries. She wore a brand new pair of patent leather Mary Janes and they stuck five little candles into her millefeuille, squashing the cream between the layers. We should have known that we were spoiling her.

You can have a Happy Meal, I said to her this time. You can get soda and even a toy.

I want Daddy, said Lulu.

We were standing in her bedroom, the walls painted an obscenely fleshy shade of pink that she had chosen herself. Now she was pulling all of her dresses out of her closet to try on. It was nearly seven PM; I had picked her up from school hours ago and we still had yet to leave the house. Why couldn't she wear her school uniform? Who had put these delusional vanities into her head? I was hungry. I had returned to my old job recently. I was working hard, I was excelling. The team had struggled without me. Plus, one of the senior strategists was set to retire, and I knew he had his eye on me as a replacement.

I'll buy you ice cream, I said.

I want French pastry, said Lulu.

Don't be pretentious, I snapped. French pastry is expensive and overrated.

Things change quickly. Shortly after Lulu's birthday last year, Ben's company terminated him for lackluster performance. Although this year I told myself that Ben was on a business trip, he was really traveling for an interview—for a job he didn't yet have and probably wouldn't get. When we had first met in college, Ben's idealism had inspired me. Now I knew that Ben's aspirations toward radicalism only manifested in inaction, ineptitude, and performative rage—which left him irritable and frequently depressed. He sat at home most days reading articles, never shutting up about late capitalism and the climate crisis, even though both had something to do with our comfortable home and affluent lifestyle.

Lulu pulled her dresses off of the bed, throwing them on the floor and kicking them.

Kick them, tear them up, I don't care, I said. A stupid little girl like you doesn't need so many dresses.

You're mean to me, she cried. I don't like you. Where is Daddy?

Lulu looked at me, her expression ferocious. I felt a pang in my stomach. I did not realize it was disgust just then; I thought it only hunger and exasperation. I looked into Lulu's glaring eyes and saw Ben—his incompetence and conceit; how it was sucking me up, not just my earnings and my savings but my patience, my intelligence, the very vitality of my being, just like this useless daughter that I had permitted him to put inside of me.

I shut Lulu in her room with her dresses and went through the McDonald's drive-thru on my own. I ordered a double quarter pounder with cheese, twenty chicken McNuggets, large fries, and a large Coke. For Lulu, a single Filet-O-Fish. When I got home, she was lying on the floor, crying.

Don't be dramatic, I said. You're just hungry.

I left the Filet-O-Fish at her feet and went to settle down in bed. Dinner in my lap, a television show, a nice glass of wine. I loved having the master bedroom to myself—I was used to it now, even when Ben was home. He had started sleeping in the study recently, on the pull-out couch. I couldn't stand the grisly documentaries about veganism and the food industry that he had taken to watching, and in the study, he could watch them alone late into the night.

When I told my friends over brunch that we were sleeping separately, they were concerned for our marriage—but I was happy that Ben had moved. The quality and duration of my sleep had improved, and, in some respects, our marriage was better. In fact, whenever Ben did venture to disturb me in the master bedroom, sex occurred with greater ease. All he had to do was knock on the door; there were no more annoying and ambiguous caresses attempted when I was already half asleep. Although I found Ben increasingly inadequate as an individual, I had to admit that I now enjoyed having sex with him more. Back when we first met, I had been too anxious, there had been too much pressure. Sleeping with him had felt like the only avenue I had toward making him like me. Now I no longer had to worry about that—Ben depended on me for our groceries, for our Netflix subscription, for our family. He had to like me.

Only ten minutes into my show, Lulu burst into my bedroom.

Knock next time, I said.

Daddy always says eating fast-food fish makes you sick, said Lulu.

Nonsense.

Daddy said it's unsustainable and bad for our oceans.

Then don't eat it.

Lulu burst into tears.

I already ate it, she said, through hiccups. I was hungry. Can I have some chicken nuggets?

I shoved the chicken McNuggets back into the takeout bag, ignoring her request, and went to check if Lulu had finished her sandwich. On the pink butterfly carpet in her room lay the Filet-O-Fish box. It was empty. Only a smear of tartar sauce remained on its grease-stained paper lining.

If you're going to have principles, I said, you have to act on them.

Otherwise it's just pretend, like your father pretends.

Lulu wasn't listening to me. She collapsed onto her bed, clutching her stomach.

I feel so sick, she said. I have cramps.

You don't even know what a cramp is, I said to her.

You have cramps all the time, Lulu said. This is the worst birthday ever. If Daddy were here, he would have bought me French pastry and let me make a wish and blow out the candles.

It was a pathetic little performance. Lulu rolled up into a fetal position and curled her hands into fists. She let out a high-pitched whine, as if she was still a baby, as if I wasn't there, as if I hadn't wholly devoted the past six years of my life to teaching her object permanence, language processing, basic reading, and social function. As if everything was up to Daddy when really, she depended on me—even Daddy depended on me. I felt another jolt in my stomach.

I'm so sick I'm going to *throw up*, Lulu screamed.

But it wasn't her in the end—it was me. Gagging violently, I ran to the bathroom, her little footsteps slapping the floor behind me. Bile spurted out of my nostrils. All around me I could smell the salty odor of hot cheese, ketchup, pre-digested low-quality beef. Heaving into the toilet, recoiling from Lulu's soft breath on the back of my neck, I knew. I felt for a second time that new swelling in my stomach. I saw ahead of me, for many years, a long road without end.

# MICHAEL HOWRIE

*Stairwell*

You are in the house of the neighbour who always invites you in for tea, although you usually decline – until today. Today you are sitting in what he calls a parlour, which you see as a sitting room. It's arranged so neatly and compactly that every piece of furniture borders another and each object on display has no more than an inch between itself and something else. He is about ten, fifteen years older than you and talking about things you don't care about – the state of the tenement building, the noise from upstairs, the weather. Thoughts intrude upon your mind. *What if I bit his cheek; what would he do?*

'Is something the matter? Is the tea alright?'

*What if I bit him, now?* You're staring at his jowls and can feel your tongue pushing up against your teeth. You think he notices.

'Everything's fine, thanks. The tea's great.'

Your eyes wander around his parlour – his sitting room – and you search for something to make conversation out of. Everything is old and brightly coloured, but pristinely ornamental, so you pick out the one shabby thing in the room: a browned painting of a field or the sea. It's hard to make out. He is surprised that you chose it and decides to tell you its history.

Your thoughts begin to notice they're being ignored and bumble behind your forehead. *His flat is full of breakable objects.* You try to keep your gaze away from a teapot, high up on a shelf, but the harder you fight the urge the more it brings you back to the alabaster-white surface. Again and again, you see yourself taking the two steps that would be needed to swipe it to the ground; lift it and let it fall; punt it into the floorboards. *He would love it if anything were to break.*

You feel your fingers twitching with the motion of grasping it and realise you have missed the entirety of your neighbour's story about the painting. It was fascinating, you're sure. You wonder if you can keep your thoughts under better control. *What if I kissed him?* You can see yourself doing it.

'You're sure the tea's alright?' he asks you. 'I had a friend over last week that swore it was off.' He twirls his finger around his spoon. 'But how can tea go off?' He pauses. 'I'm being silly. Must've misheard.'

'You've lived here a long time, haven't you?'

Your neighbour looks up from his cup. 'Long enough to know I'm not myself anymore.'

His response strikes you. Your neighbour has always seemed obscure, but now he's making sense to you. *How would I know when I stopped being myself?*

'Do you think it's the living here that changed you or just the passing of time?' you ask him.

'Age doesn't change everyone.' He turns away. 'I don't know what did it, but I've lost the man that moved in here. He's probably rattling about under the floorboards somewhere. I don't know.'

Something in his face reminds you of a film you've seen. You thought it was sad. No, sad wasn't the right word for it – maybe mournful. Not quite mournful, but despondent. The characters were constantly moving from one desolate town to another. Your neighbour shares with them the same downward slant of his eyes and the same glum acceptance of loss. You want to ask him about it.

'If you were freezing in the dead of night, would you burn the cart that you were driving?'

He looks at you more directly now; he's almost smiling. The question seems to resonate in him in the same way that his response did in you.

'Why do I have a cart?'

'The donkey that was pulling it has died and the cart contains all of your possessions. You have to pull it now.'

'I would burn it.'

'Even without knowing how much farther you had to go?'

'I would burn it.'

You remember that that's what they did in the film. They burnt it all at once and kept walking into the desert. You wondered at the time why they didn't break it down into pieces to keep for kindling over different nights. But now you aren't sure if you would have remembered it at all if they hadn't let it burn into a blaze.

Your neighbour stands up and takes away the cups for your tea. He thanks you for coming and leads you to the door. *I should bite him now.* He is holding the door open and beckoning you through. *I should turn and bite his cheek.* He waits before closing it and looks at you in your eyes again.

'You're welcome anytime,' he says. 'I'm glad you finally took me up on the offer.'

You thank him for having you. *I should kiss him.* You suppress the thought. *I could punch him in the stomach and run.* He is still looking at you. *I'm going to crush his fingers as he shakes my hand.* You say your thanks again.

'My pleasure,' he says. He's still standing there.


You find yourself in the shadowed stairwell of the tenement building and walking down the steps. Cables of light are strewn about the walls. You look up to see his door is now closed – you don't know what you did just before leaving. Did you bite him or kiss him? Shake his hand or knee his groin?

You do know what you did. You're just playing with the possibility that maybe you forgot. The fact is you did nothing, and you didn't want to, you tell yourself. You wonder where such thoughts come from. Perhaps they crawl in through your ears or your nostrils to sit and bark behind your forehead. Maybe they come from somewhere inside, somewhere so far down that it's no longer really a part of you, to shout up from beneath the dark window.

You descend the stairs slowly, holding onto the banister. Slowly enough to close your eyes for a moment and feel about for where your mind is. You start behind your lids, in that dim, hazy swim of black colours. If you want, you can pull the focus up higher, between your temples. You drag your consciousness down instead, towards your jaw, but the curve of the banister tells you to open your eyes again and turn onto the next landing. *I could slip and fall at any moment.*

You rarely give much thought to who you are anymore. You used to obsess about those questions when you were a child: of the boundary of the self, of the reality of imagination, of how you see yourself and how the world sees you. *What if I fell and knocked out all my memories?*

You used to lie awake at night and imagine all the other people in the world that would be lying awake at night and imagining you. You had thoughts about travelling and travelling through time – if the Earth just kept spinning wouldn't a jump in time leave you stranded in space? You once made a note of the hour and the date to give yourself an anchor to travel back to without causing too much surprise. *I could scream and wake the neighbours.*

You try to remember when that You went away. Maybe you suppressed it until all its inward-facing thoughts became compacted and tiny enough to resurface now as intruders. You are nearly on the ground floor. The stairwell is still dim, but you have adjusted to the gloom and can pick out the colours of the walls and the floor. Dark green tiles, faded cream paint, horribly greasy knobs at the corners of the bannisters. The noises of neighbours living behind closed doors echo down the stairwell.

The taste of the tea is still in your mouth. It has become too bitter to bear, and you now think that it was off. You don't know how tea can go off.

You reach the bottom step and walk down the dark corridor to the heavy front door of the tenement building. You click the lock open and step into the weak sunlight, and your thoughts fall away. You return to yourself by acting unconsciously or you leave yourself by forgetting your own mind, and the day goes on, and the wind in your face doesn't care who you are now.

## EILEEN VANDERGRIFT

*Enough*

A stiletto-legged heron
slurps small silver fish
                    head first,
canapés from the sterling tray
sun can make of water.

Each morning rising,
                    blue or gray
—depending on the light—
                    blue or gray
not needing to say
            for sure

that delicate chandelier
        alighting reedy edges
            stalks with grace
                without apology.

## EILEEN VANDERGRIFT

*The morning we gathered to*
*bury Tom, who was 24*


A call goes out to every corner of our house
                    pelicans have been spotted trolling the lake
a momentary full stop—
                    every landscape changing.

Each of us pauses
                    face to different window
small children, pressed against glass
                    swollen with Christmas longing.

This is a moment when the bird's story is our own
                                        and everyone else's we love.

Pelicans, those squat, feathered sailboats, bob and fish,
filling their bills with loot enough to carry them south toward survival
                    while I picture cartoon robbers with large canvas bags—

So we came together that October morning
                    bent before the long migratory path ahead
                    where no destination could yet be divined

still    and still together in the calamity of reshaping family.

I will remember the pelicans when children skate

upon this liquid world come winter.

I will remember that the liquid world is only one season.

I will remember the lake

migration's brutal demands
time's thread suturing those seasons
binding us to Tom
and every life that's called us home.

# EILEEN VANDERGRIFT

*I'm not one of those people*

who believes
there's no such thing as a stupid question.
It's like insisting there's no such thing
as solid water.

There are questions that display
how little you were listening,
Greyhound's tagline repurposed
*Leave the thinking to us.*

There are questions dressed in red fedoras
or black silk stockings, seams rounding each calf,
seductive reflections
         no question at all once the pleasing echo's passed.

Then there are those questions that jump into the deep end
         absent any effort to learn how to swim
         looking to be carried ashore—
         a listener's 'mouth to mouth', your plan for survival.

All these conditions inspire stupid questions,
answers mere coins dropping between a car's seats
or from a torn pocket through water.
         Solid answers need a ledge to land on.

         Your own questions
       the ones worth asking, have no answers
     have no chance of going away,
will be with you forever.

*Aisle Five*

Ruth stares at the loosely plastic-wrapped cauliflower with little interest. It is dented from all sides and its leaves are wilting, closing in on each other. She transfers this sad-looking ball into her trolley and drags her sturdy brown boots over to the fruit aisle. Again, a few ripe bananas breathing in their own recycled air. Then she rifles through five varieties of potatoes, and after a moment of consideration, chooses one. Ron, her son, is coming home from university today. He is not coming alone.

When she and Tim had driven Ron for his first week at university, their car was filled up to its neck with ten cartons and two extra-large suitcases, one brass lamp, three posters in support of Arsenal, and five Tupperware boxes of frozen meals that Ron could heat up anytime. At the last minute, Ruth had stuffed in the gingham blanket Ron used to love when he was five. Her son had insisted that he didn't want to take it, but Ruth had stuck it into the bottom of his suitcase anyway. A few weeks into September, when filled by a large burst of homesickness, Ron had called up Ruth. His voice was shaky as though he had been crying – he claimed he had contracted something called freshers' flu – and he told Ruth that he found the blanket.

In those early months, Ron took the train home often to eat Ruth's famous shepherd's pie, or spend time with their dog, Bruno. At Ruth's office, her fellow colleagues – one of whom had a magnet on her desk, 'Mother first, Architect later' – were bent on giving her unsolicited advice. They told her that this would all change soon – that the kids eventually get over this longing for home – that they get over you. Soon enough, Ron's visits lessened over time. On one break, he said he had too much work at university, and that he was going to run for captaincy of the rugby team. On another, there was a fantastic ten-day trip planned to the Highlands.

After a particularly sour dinner last year, however, the visits had come to a stop altogether.

Ron had come home for his nineteenth birthday, and he brought his buddy, Nathan. Ron and Nathan were tight. They were on the rugby team together. It was Nathan who helped Ron out when his project went missing from his laptop, and it was Nathan's sister who helped get him the internship at the BBC – remember, Mum? – *Nathan* was the one with whom Ron had celebrated his eighteenth birthday. *Nathan*. Then just after Ron blew out his birthday candles, nine due to lack of space, and one for good luck, he held Nathan's hand in his, and told his parents that Nathan was more than just a friend.

Ruth walks across to the next aisle – aisle five – which Ruth thinks of as dairy heaven. She sees tubs of feta, Camembert, cheddar, pecorino, and is tempted to pick them all. She had originally been planning to make a spinach, cheese and mushroom quiche for dinner, but Ron had already messaged twice reminding her that Nathan has turned vegan. Regardless, Ruth throws a big block of cheese to the top of her pile. She can't just accept everything. Thinking about her son with another boy makes her stomach tighten and her breath sharp. Like the night that Ron blew out his birthday candles, including the one for good luck. Both she and Tim stood there, laughing at first at their now-adult son's weird sense of humour. They didn't always understand it, but they laughed along anyway. Ruth noticed, after clearing the table and another round of wine, that Ron was still holding that boy's hand tightly in one hand and biting the nails of the other. She stopped, her stomach taut, her breath heavy, her feet numb. Then she picked up an obscenely large piece of cake, went into her room, and did not come back out. Tim followed.

Months after that dinner of not speaking about it – with each other and with their son – Ruth and Tim had decided to call Ron home to clear things up. Nothing that a good shepherd's pie couldn't fix. They had hoped Ron wouldn't bring up the topic of Nathan again – that it was just a phase that would have passed. They were taken aback when Ron mentioned bringing Nathan along.

Right now, walking towards this aisle is a young woman asking everyone to excuse her. Ruth observes her while she struggles to balance a few items on her arms. She has neither a trolley nor a basket, and Ruth is worried that the box of eggs will slip and crack on the floor. She doesn't, however, offer to help. The girl dangerously adds a pack of bananas on to her arm, and the pile shudders. She is walking closer to Ruth now. She is young and has skin the colour of charred toast. And her eyelashes are long and – a word that isn't coming to Ruth's mind just yet.

'Gorgeous!' Ruth hears a sound beside her. She turns and sees that the girl is speaking to her. 'Your scarf is gorgeous!' She reaches over, now knocking down the bananas, and touches the edge of Ruth's scarf with ease.

'Thank you. It's pashmina,' Ruth says, elongating the first half of the word too much, with the unfamiliarity of someone who has only ever read the word and never heard it.

The girl with the pile laughs. 'Lovely. Pashmina.' She repeats the word, only a little differently.

'Oh. Am I saying it wrong?' Ruth turns towards her.

'A bit. It's just pashmina. A soft *a*. Like the word rush. Or lush,' says the girl.

Lush. That's the word Ruth was looking for. Looking at her, Ruth is reminded of her roommate at university, Lila. Lila and Ruth would sit for hours leaning in front of their low-lit mirror and attempt to curl their eyelashes using coconut oil and a warm spoon, with little result. Lila didn't need to do this, though. She was blessed with long lashes and dark, shapely eyebrows even before people began fiddling with theirs. Ruth wonders what Lila is doing these days. She hasn't thought about her in so long. She remembers how Lila would stay up with Ruth on the night before a big assignment and make tons of coffee for the two of them. 'Why are you having this much coffee? I'm the one who is stressed out!' Ruth would say, nose burrowed in blueprints and plans. 'Well, watching you stress stresses me out! And that's what good friends do – they worry together,' Lila would grin, the gap in her front teeth visible – a feature that Ruth found both ugly and interesting. She remembers that when Lila would be asleep, Ruth would sometimes slip her fingers into her own pyjamas and touch herself. When Ruth got married to Tim, for a long time afterward she thought about Lila. She thought about the gap in her teeth, which Ruth didn't find so ugly anymore. And she thought some more about Lila. Then one day, she forgot.

At the till, Ruth hands her shopping over. 'Is that all, love?' the man says, throwing the items into a Tesco bag. Ruth says yes. The clumsy girl arrives at the adjacent counter, and releases the big stash from her arms. She catches Ruth's eye and smiles. No gaps. Ruth looks away. A moment later, she asks the man if he could keep aside the block of cheese. Tonight, she decides, she can do without it.

*The Problem with Trumpets*

He didn't enjoy the music they played in this café. He much preferred classical, not classic rock, but that's also why he sat here to do his work. It forced his focus inward, to the space behind his forehead but in front of the skinfolds on the back of his bald head.

His table was at the front, centered in the large window. People avoided it because the chill from outside seeped through the glass and under their skin, only noticeable when all the hair on their arms stood raised beneath their sweater in warning. He didn't mind; leaving his jacket on saved him the trouble of taking it off.

The best part of this café was his routine. Every day at 3:00 P.M., sometimes 3:02 P.M. if he got caught up in choosing a scarf, he settled himself at his table by the window, accounting for time outside the café to have a smoke at 2:55 P.M. His briefcase took an impolite seat in the adjacent chair after he retrieved his work. The score sat open in front of him on the table, pages ready to turn, while black, blue, and pink pens waited to be chosen. The tea he ordered, always black tea, was centered above the score on the other half of the table. By 3:15 P.M. he finished the first cup, warming his bloodstream back to room temperature after the cold walk from his apartment to the café, only half a block. The trick was to have multiple orders of the smaller portion of tea; he always beat the chill from the window to the bottom of the cup.

There were only five other tables in the café, though he usually didn't notice the other occupants. The outside framing of the café was blue, but it was the kind of blue that made the sky uncomfortable because it couldn't live up to the paint. It was a touristy part of town, and bright colors were expected. They made people excited, made them feel as if they were visiting somewhere new that had never before been seen. Across the street was a pub, golden lights behind deep burgundy curtains. The gold cursive of the sign stretched above the doorframe was missing a letter: "The oyal Pub." He hated that pub and that missing letter. It got into his head, caused chaos with the possibility of the timpani staying silent on a downbeat that should instead be full.

It was 3:02 P.M. He settled in, picked up the blue pen, and began counting, peering over his glasses at the score while the pen steadily counted the beats in a dance through the air. He hesitated every once in a while, pausing to jot a note or circle a problem, but his hand quickly returned to hovering, conducting an orchestra only he could hear.

The fat under his chin was bothering him. It kept distracting the hand that turned the pages of the score. A new mole sat on the skin there; he'd discovered it that morning upon a cursory glance in the mirror. He couldn't remember what it looked like, but his fingers kept returning to bother it as if it were a scab that he could slough off in favor of the redness it would leave behind. But the real problem was that the horn section was always off in this section of the piece. Somewhere in these eight bars, it didn't all fit. He'd determined the horns were the problem only after eliminating the possibility that the violins were at fault. He could hear it now: the trumpets. The whole piece could be ruined by eight bars that didn't fit and then that would be the end of it.

He tilted his head up, searching for harmony in the corner where the window and the wall and the ceiling met. A passing umbrella distracted his gaze, sending the trumpets whirling out of control. A face in an apartment window across the street was witness to his predicament. The woman was old, wrinkles hanging on her face made more apparent by her extreme stillness and lack of expression. Her white hair sat in loose curls on her head, though he suspected it was a wig. His bald scalp hissed with a chill from the window.

She was right above the missing letter, as if she could make up for its absence with her presence at the window. A burgundy lampshade, tilted askew, gave the bottom of her face an eerie glow, lighting her throat which hung in loose strips, as if she didn't have enough strength to support her own skin. He wondered if the books piled on the windowsill were hers. If so, she must have read them because they held zero interest for her eyes. She was captivated by the rain, watching the bobbing and weaving of umbrellas passing on the street below. He didn't realize how long he'd been staring until she blinked, slowly, as if taking her time would prolong her death. This blink exposed that she was, in fact, staring directly at him and had been for some time. His fingers scratched at his mole self-consciously. She must see it there on the fat beneath his chin, and maybe she stared because it made his already thin mouth seem thinner.

He flipped back a few pages in the score, starting at the beginning of the section. The violins had a lyrical melody, slowly building the rest of the symphony into their chorus. The pen flounced in the air, its graceful pattern stumbling once again upon the entrance of the horns, surprised each time by their blare. He pursed his lips, wondering if the pull of skin would stretch the mole and make it look bigger. Maybe the trombones were the problem, except his pen didn't stop when they began their drone; it was only upon the entrance of the trumpets, but he couldn't eliminate their statement. Maybe they simply needed mutes.

The smell of stale smoke crawled through the window. He turned toward it instinctively, but he couldn't smoke again so soon. The woman was still watching him from the window. He couldn't tell if she was breathing, but knew she must be or she wouldn't be able to stand so purposefully still. He couldn't see anything but her head from this angle, her body blocked by the windowsill and rain between them, which was more of a mist but enough precipitation to cause the window to fog, blurring the edges of her face. She almost looked like his wife through the blur, or at least, what he remembered his wife had looked like years ago before she passed. She would've noticed the mole earlier, would've batted him down the street to the doctor with her cane, *tsk*ing her tongue against her teeth between lectures about smoking and eating and health. The woman in the window, who wasn't his wife, must be listening to music, he decided; there was no other explanation. His fingers were cold, and the mole felt like it had grown.

He began conducting again, pen gripped tightly between his fingers. They might've turned white if they weren't already red with cold. He adjusted the scarf around his neck, wishing it could reach high enough to cover the mole. The mole had likely been there for quite some time, his eyes choosing to ignore it so he could ignore his dead wife who wouldn't have allowed him to ignore the doctor. He could feel it with every swallow as if its roots extended into his throat. He had begun to take breaths more often. Maybe that was why he was cold, breathing too much air from the window. She was still watching him but he didn't dare pull his eyes from the score on the table. His page-turning hand reached for his cup of tea. Its chill soothed his worried throat.

The trumpets had to be eliminated. He couldn't hear another way for them to fit besides not at all. They were too loud, blaring over the rest of the symphony in the crass way that only trumpets can achieve. His eyes betrayed him, stealing to the window and across the street. Cymbals crashed and his pen fell, surprised ink betraying the page. The lamp was still lit and the books sat untouched, but the woman was gone; the mole relaxed back into his skin.

He packed his briefcase with unsteady hands, fingers stiff with a chilled inability to remember how to bend. Tea was left unfinished though steam no longer colored the air above the cup. His scarf was wrapped perhaps too tightly around his neck, pulled up uncomfortably high to cover the mole; he didn't want to see it in shop window reflections. He lit a cigarette and shuffled down the street on his way home, the ghost of mortality quietly settling under his skin with every inhale. He ignored it; the trumpets were silenced for now.

ZHANGLU WANG

*Family*

Rock candy splutters in the oil; the hissing and the splashing make her take a step back. As the candy melts into the brown liquid, she adds pork chops and chopped garlic to it. A sweet smell of sugar, meat and spices instantly rises, and she covers the pan to let it simmer. The kitchen ventilator is making a lot of noise and she cannot hear what her husband and Keke are saying in the living room clearly, but from the noise they are making, it seems like they're having a heated discussion.

She smiles. Her husband has woken Keke up.

Their daughter Keke is back home for the winter holidays. As usual, the girl lay down on the sofa and placed an open book on her face when she arrived at home earlier today, saying, "I'm so sleepy, Mom. Please wake me up for dinner."

She took the book away with a motherly tenderness when Keke fell asleep, and covered her with a light quilt. She looked at her daughter as she slept. A beautiful girl, long brows, a thin nose, plump and rosy cheeks, full lips.

A spoiled child, everyone said.

Keke *is* spoiled, she thinks, while cooking. She knows that pork chops are Keke's favorite, so no need for anybody to mention it, she is cooking it for Keke. But Keke hasn't learned to cook herself, which is worrying.

"No man would want a woman that doesn't cook," she'd told Keke many times. How did Keke reply?

"No worries." Keke had been watching TV, and she had said the same thing as she always did. "I'll find a partner better than yours. He'll cook for me."

Keke's father was sitting next to her, and hearing this, he protested: "I also cook."

"You don't," said Keke. The conversation was over.

The pork chops are a brown color. She slides them onto a plate and decorates it with broccoli. Setting the plate on the table outside the kitchen, on which she's already laid fried cabbage with tofu, steamed sweet potatoes, seasoned shrimp meat, she calls, "Time for dinner."

Keke and her father come to the table and sit down. The table is well lit by the lamp above them. She looks at the food and is proud of how well it has turned out.

Keke taps her fingers on the table. It looks like she is meditating.

"Mom, could you please lend me your phone? I need to check my grades. They should be out by now."

"You can't do it with your phone?"

"It's charging by the sofa."

She gives Keke her phone.

"What's your password, Mom?"

"You know I don't have one."

Keke smiles. "Why not?"

"I don't need it."

"But your husband has one," Keke lowers her head.

For a moment she wonders why Keke has picked this topic. She knows that her husband has a password. He didn't always, but one day she tried to borrow his phone to look up a recipe when hers wasn't at hand, and she found that she couldn't access it like she usually could. She asked him, and he snatched his phone away and said, "What's the thing you want to look up?"

He said it like it was no big deal, so she believed it.

"I hold a decent position in the company," the father says now. "I need to make sure the information in my phone is secure."

"Oh, yes, 'the information,'" Keke giggles.

"I'm telling you this," he sounds angry. "It's impolite to question your father."

"I didn't mean to." Keke keeps giggling. "I just wanted to check my grades."

Neither of them has taken anything from the plates in front of them since the conversation began, and the food is now losing its heat in the winter evening. She feels really bad for herself. It's always like this. She spends a whole hour cooking, and they don't take the food seriously.

"Could you stop talking? You're supposed to *eat* at dinner time."

Keke puts the phone on the table. "Sure."

The first dinner of welcoming Keke home from university isn't going as she expected, and she is disturbed by it. Aware of her bad mood, Keke offers to wash the dishes when they finish. The husband goes to the main bedroom, where he can watch TV while staying in his quilt. She goes to the big balcony to collect the clothes that have been dried by the sun, and then enters the bedroom to put the clothes away. Though exempt from the cold water and greasy plates, there's always something more for her to do. She's used to it.

On the television a historical drama is playing. A story happening in a time when people referred to ancient texts to express their love, a time when language had a high emotional density. She is folding a shirt, sitting on the side of the bed, watching the main couple confess to each other as they are forced to separate. Her husband is half-lying, half-sitting in the center of the bed, wrapped up like a silkworm chrysalis.

"*Having seen the vastness of the ocean, any water I come across since cannot compare with it. You are the one for me, and I will never fall in love again after knowing you,*" the male lead says.

"*When the mountain edges are lost and the rivers are exhausted, when the thunder shakes in winter and the snow falls in summer, when the sky and the earth unite, that is the time when I dare not be with you.*" The female lead echoes his affection.

"Why did you get a password?" she asks, suddenly.

Her husband's explanation would have made sense, but she knows that he has stayed in the same position in the company for many years. The password has been there for only one month. Maybe two months.

"What?" He's still watching TV, but as he realizes what she's just asked, he focuses on her, and puts on an angry expression. "Keke likes to start trouble, I thought you knew that. You shouldn't be asking this stupid question."

"I'm asking this stupid question, because your answer was even more stupid."

He doesn't reply. In that silkworm chrysalis he makes a clumsy jump so that he can turn his back to her. In order to keep watching the drama, he twists his neck to an impossible angle, and says, "Don't talk to me."

She puts all the clothes into the closet and leaves the room without uttering one word. She goes to the kitchen. Keke is still there, washing the dishes while listening to music on her headphones.

"Don't listen for too long. It's bad for your ears."

"Okay." Keke takes a slow glance at her and speaks with a voice louder than usual.

She goes into the small balcony near the kitchen, where she has dipped her and her husband's clothes in water. The clothes are in a big basin. She identifies a piece of black fabric from the mess. His underwear. She is suddenly irritated.

"Keke," she calls.

Keke comes to her.

"I just quarreled with your father, and I don't want to wash his underwear," she says. "You wash it when you finish the dishes."

Keke looks amused.

"If you want to punish him, you leave his underwear untouched until the day he finds out that he has nothing to wear," Keke says. "He wouldn't care who washes them, as long as somebody does."

"You don't want to wash them?"

Keke shakes her head and leaves.

She sighs. She looks at the underwear. It's his underwear, but the only thing he does with them is wear them. It is she who bought them and washes them every time, and of course it's her duty to wash them *today*. She takes the soap.

When she finishes she goes into the living room. Keke is there, watching the same drama as her father on the second TV set. After parting from his lover, the male lead has met another woman. On their first meeting, she lifts her chin and speaks with an arrogant voice: "Who are you?" And he smiles. The lighting makes it look like the sunshine of the city all falls on him.

*Romance warning,* she thinks.

"Milk?" Seeing her, Keke lifts a mug she prepared for her mother. Hot, sweet-scented milk.

She believes that Keke has put rock candy in it. "How come you boiled milk tonight? You used to have me do it for you."

"I think you need a hot drink after washing the clothes. Your hands must be cold," Keke says. "Like mine."

She smiles and takes the mug.

"Thank you."

*A Grave Matter*

'Tis about seven o'clock that morning.

Robert Downes has barely slept, so acute is his anticipation. He leaves his bedroom in darkness and walks towards the Meadows by a meandering scenic route: through the Grassmarket, up the West Bow, tarrying beneath the castle and cathedral. Downes starts down George IV Bridge, stopping there awhile. He is not yet tired of the view from the new construction. So much of the city is changing. So much of the world. His heart is heavy. His mind racing, hastily drafting involuntary lines. A couplet.

> *So that our feet shall not mix with dirt,*
> *Man raiseth his streets o'er the Earth.*

Downes repeats the couplet, counting out the syllables with his fingers. Are they a regular metre? He is uncertain. What is the next line? Should he prove his worth, or perhaps build a hearth … Does the phrase 'heaven's hearth' mean anything? After giving the matter careful consideration, Downes supposes that sadly, no, it probably does not.

He wonders if his thoughts need a variation in metre; sonnet form, perhaps. He tries fragmenting his feelings into two alternating rhyming patterns that play off each other, allowing their sounds and meanings to contrast for comical or profound effect. The attempt is futile and gives him a headache. He sits down.

The sun rises on Greyfriars. Downes points to the graveyard. '*Mortality! Thou speakest!*' he declares with theatrical astonishment. He takes unsteadily to his legs, his arm outstretched towards the graveyard.

Downes has lived in the city for three years now. He is well aware of where Greyfriars is located, even in the dark. He walks amongst the tombs muttering to himself: Byron, Shakespeare, Blake. When the daylight is inarguable, he steels himself and marches to the Meadows.

Professor George McGonagall rises at six. He tells his wife that he has important business to attend to. He kisses her farewell, assuring his return by evening meal time. He has three daughters. He says goodbye to them all. He then meets his coachman, Andrew Kinnaird, at the gates of his house. Kinnaird doffs his cap and mutters the word 'sir'. He is ready, just as he said he would be. Kinnaird flashes the two muzzle-loading pistols he has procured. McGonagall nods dutifully and silently enters the coach.

They ride towards the city. McGonagall allows a moment for quiet tears. He reminds himself that this is duty. This is the blessed process of superseding. It is necessary. Without this process, there is no progress. The germs of a poem begin forming in his mind: process/progress, civilisation needing/superseding. Is there any potential in this as a composition?

No, he concludes.

Not really.

The grievance between them issued two days previously, at a public lecture. McGonagall had been invited to speak on modern poetry. As he was a renowned professor in the city of Edinburgh, the hall was crowded with attendees – whose hearts were light and free of sorrow.

Amongst the thronged faces, McGonagall spied his former student. Their relationship was close. Downes often visited the professor's office to debate the classics; tentatively, they had begun sharing their own writing between themselves.

A moment of wild candour had led the professor to call out to Downes that day, publicly proclaiming the brilliance of the young man's writing. Downes, as deferential as he was irradiant, had disputed the claim and insisted on the superiority of the professor's work.

'*I never meant to hurt you, speaketh vice unto to virtue.* How can a man not weep at such words?' McGonagall had shouted.

'You make beauty from science, sir,' Downes replied. '*We are here not from God, but providence. Like otters, trees, and cormorants.'*

They quoted each other's words further, though soon their voices were lost amongst the laughter of the thinning crowd.

It had been a mortal humiliation.

McGonagall knew this day would be remembered, for a very long time. His reputation, his authority, the trust in his aesthetic judgements was publicly undermined.

In the heat of the moment he had demanded the duel – to reclaim lost honour, aye, but also to conclusively settle the matter of who indeed was Edinburgh's greatest living poet.

McGonagall's coach arrives at the Meadows. Kinnaird disembarks and opens the carriage door. The professor exits with a mournful sigh.

The Meadows are dry that morning, the grass frozen. Downes stands some way off, beneath a tree, his face contorted by frustration. As Kinnaird and McGonagall approach, they hear him utter, 'I suppose now it is no matter.'

'Well met, sir,' exclaims McGonagall. 'I confess, I was uncertain of finding you here.'

'Truth and bravery are kin, sir. A host of rectitudes have my back. My heart is pure, my hands are steadied.' Downes would demonstrate the fact, but he feels their tremors.

'Lo, then, your kin protect me too. Truth is my sole preserve. As for bravery: here I stand, setting the challenge, but doing so with compassion in my heart. I offer one final opportunity for your repentance and rescinding of your comments.'

'A generous offer, sir, befitting of your august personage. However, you know I cannot do so. I stand by my words as though they were a most precious lover. You, sir, are the greatest wordsmith in this city. Far better than I.'

'Sacrilege!' The professor's voice near breaks. 'Your words move me like no other. In profession, I am master and you the student, but in reality, I have nothing to teach you of feeling, of love. The expression of the soul cannot be taught; you have the gift! I beseech you, sir, see sense. Repent.

Else my most remarkable contribution to this literary world may be to deprive it of a flowering genius.'

'Master, please, it is I who risks depriving the world of beauty. Your words are honeyed logic. You are Newton and Shakespeare, expressed as one. And if you are Newton, I – I simply squat at your feet, hoping for beautiful crumbs to obey your law.'

With both men refusing to concede, Kinnaird brings forth the pistols and presents them one apiece. Initially Kinnaird was to stand only as the professor's official second, yet Downes had no one prepared to act as his and so Kinnaird now stands for them both. The poets have co-authored an official statement, declaring their intention to duel, and their willing compliance in the endeavour whatever the consequences. All three sign the statement; they do so weeping and embracing.

Kinnaird supervises the loading of the pistols with powder and lead balls. He positions the poets back to back, pistols raised to chest height. Kinnaird clears his throat.

'Dearest gentlemen. We are here today to resolve an issue of great honour and dignity. I will now count to twenty. Each number represents a step you must take forwards. Once the twentieth step has been taken, you must turn and fire your shot. Understood?'

The poets confirm comprehension. Kinnaird begins to count, slowly. As the count reaches double figures, the poets' hands are visibly shaking. As Kinnaird commands the fifteenth step, he hears McGonagall emit a sharp gasp. At sixteen, Downes's knees seem to shake. Seventeen. Eighteen. Nineteen. The men visibly stiffen. The word twenty is simply that – a word. It is the same as the last, nineteen, and yet Kinnaird cannot help but pause. When the word emerges, it is quivering and weak.

The poets make their final step. They turn. It is impossible to know who is faster; their shots near-simultaneous, like grounded fireworks. The air is filled with the smell of gunpowder.

Both men crumple. McGonagall falls, silently, backwards and sideways. Downes cries out in pain as he falls to his knees and then collapses forwards.

Kinnaird is confounded by their accuracy. He had made assumptions that neither man would prove proficient at arms, that perhaps, at the worst, one of them might sustain a minor graze. He rushes first to his friend and master. Death has not relaxed the professor's grip on the pistol; it points still at his own chest where he has shot himself in the heart at close range. The blood pools out across the white of his shirt. He surely perished on impact. Such moral clarity! Such nobility!

However, Kinnaird cannot comprehend how Downes has also fallen. Kinnaird then races to the dying man and asks what has befallen him. Downes drops his pistol and rolls to look upwards at the coachman, pointing to a shot clumsily executed in his stomach. He is panting, trying for words. Kinnaird deduces what has transpired. There can be no other explanation. Downes too has shot himself.

'The ... the ... professor. Does he live?' Downes manages.

Kinnaird cannot speak the truth. He crouches and nods, cradling the dying man's head. Downes is trying to say something else. Kinnaird leans in, begging the poet to repeat his final words.

'*Then ... I depart from this ... this dingy earth. Light the ... fires, in ... in heaven's hearth.*'

# TODD WORKMAN

*Winter Locomotion*

Lines of people
chug forward,

some whistle; others go
silently but for their shoes

scraping tracks onto
slush-strewn paths,

leaving frozen
sparks behind,

breath steaming
in streams,

exhausted prayers
exhaled to dissipate

halfway to heaven.

TODD WORKMAN

*Transcendence*

The sun swung through
the window in just such a way
that the steam rising up

from the porcelain sink
glowed gold, hummed
with amber music

and whispered
smoky hushes.

*Company*

The ghost would follow the girl through the house, drawn first like a cat to the jingle of her bracelets and then enchanted by the colors of her skirts. She did not object to the attention. He liked the way she belched in private, slammed desk drawers and tossed clothes about her room. The flurry of action delighted him. She liked the way he hardly spoke. Sometimes they would sit together by the old TV, watching stiff-haired men and long-legged women crackle across the screen while she ate saltines with jam. He would eye the bright compote with interest, but she never offered to share.

One afternoon, with the house expecting company, the girl found herself recruited to chop vegetables for dinner. This put her in a foul mood; she detested both work and vegetables. The ghost sat opposite her at the kitchen table, enjoying the way the chair rocked beneath his very slight weight. As with all his pleasures, it was a secret one. The girl kept few secrets.

"I am miserable," she declared. "What a day."

"But the peppers are so yellow," said the ghost.

"If only you knew how they tasted," she said. "But I wish you wouldn't whisper like that; I can hardly hear a word you say." She carried on chopping, a furrow between her brows. The ghost watched the yellow ribbons fall aside one by one.

"What are peppers like?" he wanted to know. It was the first question he'd asked in hundreds of years.

"Terrible," said the girl. "Try for yourself." She pushed a sliver toward him. It took the ghost a few attempts to stop it slipping through his hands, but at last he managed to raise the piece of pepper to his mouth. He ate delicately.

"It's been such a long time since I had any food," he told her. "I feel a little strange, I think."

"You seem improved," she noted. "Your voice isn't so quiet. And your cheeks look a little pink. Here; have some more."

"Won't your mother be upset?" He'd been raised, from what he could remember, with manners, and he felt that this was also worth a question.

"There'll be plenty to eat. What's a pepper or two? Anyways, I normally feed mine to the dog under the dinner table."

After eating the chopping board clean, the ghost was in high spirits and had developed a ringing laugh.

"You've become rather sociable!" the girl remarked with some distaste. "Why don't you join us at dinner tonight? All my uncles are in town, and they always ask me about my lessons. I'd be grateful for someone to distract them."

The ghost, usually ruled by shyness and good sense, had grown reckless from the vegetables.

"I'll come," he said, "although I'm out of practice at speaking to strangers."

By evening he had started to regret his promise.

"I'm afraid they won't approve of me," he confessed, while the girl pored over her jewelry. "How should I behave?" She seemed, after all, to be full of answers.

"Don't worry too much," she assured him. "You'll be fine. Just mind that your handshake's firm."


The meal did not begin smoothly. The ghost's voice had become quiet again, and his nerves were heightened by his struggle to keep hold of the cutlery. As he longed for the murmuring static of the television, the uncles and the mother stared down the table.

"You haven't told us how you and your friend met," the mother prompted.

"He haunts the upstairs," replied the girl.

"How interesting," said the mother, who did not approve of haunting.

"It's a lovely place you have," said the ghost.

"What's that, son?" boomed an uncle. "You'll have to speak up."

The ghost lowered his head and pondered his plate of food, for which his excitement had not been extinguished. He could feel the dog beating its tail in anticipation beneath the table. With both hands and some effort he managed to lift a forkful of potatoes. Upon the first bite, he noticed some of his earlier courage revive; with a stronger grip on the silverware he turned to the steak pie.

"Hasn't the weather just been horrid?" said the mother.

"A dreadful storm," an uncle agreed.

"Flowers all lifted out of their pots," added another.

"Blew our paper boy clean off his bike," chimed a third. "Hasn't been seen since."

"Well, there are worse things," said the ghost, discovering the glass of wine at his elbow. "I quite like drifting about in the wind."

"How interesting," said the mother, who did not approve of either drifting or wind.

"Looks like you've found yourself some kind of poet, my dear," said one monobrowed uncle to the girl. The ghost eyed a heavy casserole of yams, which gleamed just out of reach. "Which reminds me"—the brow lowered— "that your mother has told us you're failing English at school."

"Oh," the girl batted her hand, "enough about me. Do you know my friend here has been dead for centuries?"

"Now!" clapped the uncle, turning to the ghost. "You don't say. And how have you applied yourself to all that time? Being able to apply oneself is an invaluable asset, as I've often told my niece."

These seemed like strange, riddling words to the ghost, whose cheeks were becoming quite rosy. "Mainly I like to rustle in curtains and watch the TV," he said, "but I also enjoy peppers."

"Certainly, certainly," the uncle nodded, pouring him a second glass of wine. Lessons forgotten, the girl gave the ghost a wink of thanks; then, following his gaze, she pushed the casserole toward him. He helped himself carefully, then he drank his newly poured wine, in spite of the fact that he was beginning to feel overcome by the evening's offerings. Neither could he resist the magnificent softness of a plate of rolls being passed around the table. The sparkle of the good china and the flicker of the fireplace and the glaze on the yams all addled him with enjoyment. A sensation like wooziness had taken hold by the time the uncle turned to him again, brushing bits of pie from his mustache.

"So, my boy, you haven't told us how you died. Was it painful?"

"Not terribly," the ghost replied. "It was my seventeenth birthday. I was loved to death in a whorehouse." He paused for a moment, searchingly. "I recall her name was Maribel," he said. "She was very large."

"How interesting," said the mother, who heartily disliked women named Maribel.

"An excellent tale!" an uncle exclaimed.

Was it an excellent tale? wondered the ghost. He had others—thousands! Tales of beetles who'd traversed the whole upstairs, and of wandering patches of light on the floorboards, and of where the mice took their stolen saltines. But the uncles had already begun to talk of a racehorse named Montague, by whom they'd been disappointed. The girl caught the ghost's eye and yawned until her jaw popped loudly.

As the meal ended, the uncles implored the ghost to join them for whiskey and cigarettes in the sitting room.

"Oh," he said, watching the bright hem of the girl's skirt disappear up the staircase; she hadn't been invited. "I think I'd better not." The thought of cigarettes intrigued him, but to his surprise he found that these people made him feel rather—he sifted for the word—lonely. It was something he hadn't felt in a very long time. He excused himself and followed his companion.

"Thank goodness that's over," said the girl, who had flopped onto her stomach in front of the television. "Too much small-talk for me. But you got along awfully well!"

"Will we ever have to do that again?" asked the ghost, who discovered, as he spoke, that he'd grown a little tired of questions. His voice had softened once more to a whisper as the wine's effects receded.

She pulled a pack of saltines from beneath the bed. "Don't worry," she assured him. "My uncles won't be back for another year at least."

Although a year was a slippery thing to him, the ghost took comfort in her tone of conviction. He sat at her side, enjoying the plushness of the rug and the colorful changing of channels. The warmth of the girl's company; the cool touch of glass as she passed him the jam. On the television, a man with a neatly parted mustache poured a woman a glass of pale wine. The ghost wondered if Maribel would have liked television. As he took the jam, he nearly asked.

## JULIA GUILLERMINA

*Wild Wind*

That evening, I took the bus that stops near the marketplace. I ensconced myself back on the priority seat. It had been one of the windiest days in Edinburgh: the wind had pulled and pushed me all around the town, messing with my hat, with my opened coat, making me fear my feet would leave the ground. My hurting old knee had been complaining, and I revelled in the ride.

When we arrived, the night had come, and the wind had faded.

I was not looking ahead of me; I was not observing the people going by. I was just letting my eyelids fall on my eyes, narrowing my sight to the pavement. Suddenly, I saw a bulge of Egyptian blue. The beggar's sleeping bag.

I had spotted the beggar that same morning, wrapped in his bedroll, stretching out both arms ahead of him, a paper cup in his hands. His whole body leaned in; his strong legs supported the effort, engaging his back instead of his core muscles. A future back ache.

The people around him wandered about in the market, buying vegan haggis or beeswax wrappers. Couples, families, groups of students, all eating next to each other, sharing body heat in this haven on the cold windy day. If somebody gave the beggar a coin, he shook the cup, to jog others' memories about the sound of money, the existence of money. He looked like a folk creature, half human, half sack.

I forgot about him as I have forgotten about so many beggars.

He came back to my mind with the insistence of the mad wind, the one that comes when everything settles down. The wind that ensures life does not stay the same. The wind of problems and solutions. The wild wind that made Deacon Brodie change at night. The wild wind that saved the witch of the Grassmarket from death in the gallows.

The beggar's bag was empty of the beggar's body. Next to it, a carton.

I frowned: why would he leave his sleeping bag there, under the rain? I walked on, already putting this thought into the bin of bygones, when I noticed little circles in my path. They were difficult to discern against the black stone of the paving. They were money; one penny, two pence. I turned my head left, and caught sight of the beggar's stuff again.

Where was the paper cup? The coins, freed from it, had rolled to the place they were last exchanged, just before my feet.

The seven circles looked at me with round eyes.

I managed to kneel, clumsy, gripping my cane with a shaking strength, my nerves bombarding my brain with messages of pain, and I took the red coins with my right hand. The dark flagstone was wet and sandy, and so were the coins. They were like brown stains in my wrinkled hands.

I walked back despite my limping, thinking it was important. I dropped the coins in a pile near the carton, bending my back to let them go closer to the ground. They were the beggar's only possession. Where could he be, with his sleeping bag all wet in that sandy corner next to that empty carton, in the wee small hours, where no one was to be seen? A gust came to my eyes and made me blink. Half a tear appeared in each of my eyes, and I felt uncomfortable.

It had been the wind. The wild wind had stolen the beggar. She had turned him into rain, to murmur at everyone's ear 'hiyah, hiyah, hiyah'. And I was a witness of the night.

I limped slowly through the marketplace, feeling the cold, sandy phantom touch of the wet coins in my fingers. I felt nervous, a strange panic holding my hurting knee. I tried to walk faster but my cane slipped on the wet slabs under my feet. I imagined some municipal clerk must tidy the mess up the next morning. Would the coins be there, still, or would they be swallowed by the administrative machine, transformed into numbers behind a screen?

When I passed the bridge, the Water of Leith stopped its mad torrent, and my knee stopped hurting for seven steps.

OLIVER RAYMOND

*Paw-tew-gull*

The yachts clustered round their moorings in serried ranks. Carbon-fibre and fibreglass glared, blinding hulls shot white beams with the lowering sun. In the quiet waters of the marina at Vilamoura, beloved haven to the Guinness swillers and the full English breakfast gluttons, midwinter sun blazed its course across the ripples and onto Dennis's bald, perspiring pate. The pores on his forehead and his crown oozed visibly, secreting a salty grease which seeped gradually into his sideburns. He sank deeper into the enveloping bulk of a neon orange bean bag, grinning with satisfaction as the morning's thick dusting of baby powder eased the friction of his prodigious thighs against his too-brief briefs and their humid contents.

'Gaw-jus. Ab-so-lewtly bloody gawjus,' Dennis said, to no one in particular.

A waiter leant on a rail nearby, his fingers worrying at the frayed edge of a napkin. Retirees and vacationers shuffled dismally along the waterfront, peering into the empty restaurants and up to the empty balconies of countless apartments. The windows of a Chinese restaurant's vacant dining room were plastered with images of Japanese sushi. Concrete Buddhas inexplicably flanked the entrance to a pizzeria. This was the cheap escape from winter's grey northern miseries: off-peak package deals promising a good bit of sun amongst all the dormant machinery of southern Portugal's tourist trade. Three months of the year at a time-share in the Algarve. You could do worse.

Dennis looked at the pinched faces and puckered arsehole mouths, finding himself a little bemused by all this sourness. Shuttered restaurants and empty bars were quite alright by him, and as long as the bored local staff at the unconvincingly Irish pub kept the Guinness up to him, there was naught to complain about. A quick stop-off at the supermercado had the pantry of his single bedroom flat well stocked with sardinhas swimming in olive oil, and he'd not skimped on the rosé either – the fridge was full of fat-bottomed bottles of Mateus.

In the malty embrace of his fifth afternoon pint, he found himself in a state of benevolent pity. All those poor fuckers were missing the point. Just set yourself up here in a bean bag at Murphy's, let your gullet glug down the good black stuff and roast awhile in the sun. Dennis caught a glimpse of himself in the glass of the partition by the water: *Look at this fat old malt-fed tomato!* The image brought him no small amount of satisfaction. He lingered on his reflection, grinning and admiring the deepening hue of his tightening skin. Three pints ago he'd been cooked-prawn orange. Now, nearing the bottom of his fifth, he was deeply contented to observe a rich Heinz ketchupy sheen blossoming across his thighs. This was it. The lapping sounds of sparkling waters against the deck below, the gradually warming syrupy Guinness in his mitt. No one bothering him, no pinging phone clamouring for his attention. Utter bliss.

'Bom tarde.' The hoarse cigarette rasp came from somewhere behind Dennis's left ear. This greeting was, in Dennis's state of pleasantly sozzled solitude, an unconscionable intimacy.

'Whassat?'

'It's a good afternoon to do a lot of nothing, don't you think?' the woman said.

He turned, somewhat awkwardly, squeaking around in his bean bag to behold a vision in leopard-print. She leant against a barstool, a glass of white wine dripping with condensation in her left hand. Vertiginous stilettos and a faux crocodile-skin handbag completed the picture.

'Well, I've *been* enjoying a whole *bleed*ing afternoon of perfect nothing, and now you wanna impose.' Dennis put extra effort into his vowel sounds, rounding them out with calculated annoyance. In most circumstances, he'd have resented any intrusion into his sphere of delicious oblivion. But he liked what he saw. And he knew you had to put 'em down if you wanted any chance of bedding 'em. 'Negging', it was called. His randy younger brother had sent him a YouTube video explaining the technique.

The woman smiled. She sipped her wine.

'What you after then? I've not got any euros for ya.' He grinned toothily, sliding his sunglasses down the slick sweat on the bridge of his nose, leaning forward for a better look.

No words from the woman. Just a gently spreading smile, from one corner of her leathery face to the other. Cracks appeared in the broad red expanse of her top lip. She took another sip.

'I know, you're gonna try and sell me a slot in a time-share, aren't ya?' Dennis ventured. 'You're one of them tarted-up real-estate reps right? One a them what'll try and scam ya into a couple thousand quid for three months a year in some shit-hole flat.' He couldn't be sure, but Dennis got the impression she was enjoying what was an admittedly obnoxious performance, even by his boorish standards.

'Oh no, I'm nothing of the sort. I fear real estate's rather outside my realm.' She tilted her head quizzically, leaning in as she spoke. Cigarettes melded with the unmistakable reek of discount eau de parfum. Some knock-off Chanel No. 5. 'What do they call you, meu amigo inglês?'

'The name's Dennis, luvvie. But I wonder now, what's it to ya? What're ya up to?'

'Aaah, Dennis. I knew one by that name. It's a very old name.'

'Well me grandpa was called Dennis and so me old man thought I should follow on, ya see?'

Dennis was becoming a tad perplexed. Here she was, this fit old Portuguese bird, giving him cryptic lip in near-perfect English and eating into his peace and quiet. A few gulls wheeled overhead and squawked raucously into the deepening silence.

'Yours is an old name. Old before your grandfather reached his dotage. Do you know its origins, Dennis?'

'Can't say I do, not sure I care much either.' Dennis was quickly approaching the end of his tether.

'The Romans paid for their goods with *denarius*. Come to Macedonia and you'll see they still pay in denars. You could say your name speaks of money – of riches, even. Coins falling through time.'

'Now look 'ere dearie, I'm tryna enjoy a quiet pint and roast meself silly. You're either tryna sell me summink or blow smoke up me arse. I'm not thick. And what've the bleedin' Romans got to do with Vilamoura? I thought we was in Paw-tew-gull.'

Her amusement only seemed to increase with Dennis's indignant little speech. Through the amber fog of his inebriated frustration, he felt the first stirrings of something struggling against the restrictive nylon of his briefs.

'Vilamoura's a new town, yes. Fifty years ago, people like *you* started turning up. The developers saw an opportunity, and as the denars streamed in, and the Dennises followed, the high-rises piled up around the waterfront, and then back into the hills. But the Romans were here once.'

'Bugger the Romans, whaddaya mean *people like me*? Don't you be giving me cheek now.'

'Oh I don't mean anything by it. Nothing at all.' She looked away, out past the yachts to the Atlantic beyond.

'I'm not one of those joyless expats from Sussex or Surrey you know. I'm from Essex!' he protested, mock offense written in the creases around his eyes.

She laughed gently, the sound merging with the soft roar of the surf outside the marina. The sun, lower on the horizon now, bled orange rays onto the woman's exposed midriff. Her leopard-print tank top clung tight around prominent nipples; Dennis's gaze traced the raised circles of her areolae. He didn't care if she caught him at it – in fact he rather wanted her to see his want, his growing hunger.

'They called him Bacchus. And they worshipped him here.'

'Who called who what now?'

'The Romans, Dennis. They drank in his name. Danced and drank and ate and *fucked* in his name. There are remains beneath the high-rises. Ancient villas, bathing houses. I know this.'

'What are you gettin' at eh? I can see where you're 'edding.' Dennis grinned wider, resumed his methodical process of mental disrobing.

'The Greeks knew him as Dionysus. We could see your name as a derivation no?'

'Whassat mean?'

'Dennis, Denarius, Dionysus. You can see how it all adds up, I think.'

'Not sure I do, luvvie. Can't say I care much either.' Dennis felt his heart beating faster.

'Come along now, Dennis.' She straightened her body languidly, rising from the barstool, draining her glass. She turned away from him and stepped off the deck, walked slowly out of Murphy's Irish Pub.

There was a squelching, tearing sound as Dennis peeled his bulk out of the bean bag and woozily tottered after her. She disappeared around a corner in the dusk, the click of her heels echoing off whitewashed walls.

# LOLA GAZTAÑAGA BAGGEN

*Ink Beetles*

She had seen them for as long as she remembered: small, shadowy critters that scattered around in nooks and corners and skittered along the edges of her vision. Nobody else saw them, she'd learned early on. A fat little finger pointing inquisitively, asking Mummy 'what is?' But Mummy didn't see the shiny, oil slick–coloured shells that crawled along the pink digit, up her, onto her; into her hair and her ears. Mummy, irritated, snappy. Eyes that didn't turn to look at her, but stayed firmly fixed on the laundry, the groceries, the hoover. A downturned mouth. 'Mummy, what is?' repeated, until Mummy made the tutting noise with her mouth. Once, twice, an umpteenth time, and then the questions stopped.

It was unnatural. Questions are to be asked by children, such is the law of the land, and when she grew up without them, people noticed. Not consciously, not overtly, but they knew; felt it in their little fingers and their wisdom teeth, like crows a storm. The girl was odd. *Off.* The neighbour knew it, the baker knew it, her report card knew it. *Interior*, it said, disguising revulsion as polite concern. *Has a difficult time socialising. Hasn't mastered social interactions yet.*

This was no wonder: her peers knew it too. Socialising is an act of two, a tug o' war between parties willing, and they did not want anything to do with the eerie, quiet little thing that never looked at them directly, never talked, never questioned. Her eyes were pallid and round like a fish's, and they stared intently at nothing at all as small teeth thoughtfully nursed a thin bottom lip. They rolled around in long figures of eight, circling the room and travelling along beams and curtains, but no matter how hard her classmates looked, they didn't see anything for the girl to pay such close attention to. 'What are you looking at?' again and again, turning into 'what's wrong with you, freak?' and 'get away from us' and 'Mrs Cranley, she's doing it again!'

Her classmates could not see the shiny beetles all around her, but they were there. As she grew older, they grew bolder. They emerged from the corner of her eye to crawl around in plain sight. In class, they dotted chalk 'i's and traced printed borders protecting mapped countries. Closer, closer still. They crawled around the back of a classmate's head and disappeared into soft locks of hair as if they had sunk into her skull. She'd watch them creep closer, dropping from scrunchies and butterfly clips onto the pages of her notebook, skittering across the thin blue lines until she was almost bent double over her desk. And then, a finger, thinner now, still pale pink, reaching out and squishing the shiny little bead into the paper. Eyes widening and a soft exhale of breath as her finger sank into nothing but sticky pitch black, now smeared across her schoolwork.

Ink. Dark and slick like an oil spill.

She grew accustomed to looking out for the dark and black in the world; wondered if the dark smudges along Mummy's lash line had once been crushed-up little critters; if the spindly lines of trees against the deep purple sky at dusk would, upon closer inspection, reveal themselves to be clamouring masses of them, and then crumble into thousands of beetles like a windfall, or a flood. Her eyes, once pale and empty, grew dark, soaking in the black like a sponge. She read book after book, running her fingers along the muted letters as if trying to absorb them into her skin; crossing her eyes so they squirmed and squiggled almost as the creatures did. She'd whisper to herself as she read, feeling their little legs climb her arms and scale her knees like endless little pinpricks.

Mummy was now the one asking questions. Concerned tears and 'what is wrong with you?' and 'please, Maggie, just talk to me!', but she was the one not answering, dismissing, otherwise preoccupied. The report said so too, and Mrs Cranley, older now, speaking of therapy and treatments and seeing the doctor, as her classmates took to avoiding her altogether.

It didn't matter. The beetles on her page danced and circled to form words, worlds, wonders. Her fingers dipped into their crunchy little shells, time after time, and dragged lines across her cheeks and lips; rubbed smudges into her hair and the collar of her dress; wrote streams of incomprehensible truth onto paper and wood. Nobody else saw them, but she did. She understood, more than Mummy and her nervous fits, or school with its rules and rituals, or classmates who didn't care about the twisted little legs of beetles made of ink, or magic, or anything but *Yu-Gi-Oh!* or television.

Autumn stretched into winter as seven turned to eight and then nine. School ended later, the sun set sooner. The sky shimmered indigo. Dark and slick like an oil spill; children laughed in the distance as they ran along to play, to soccer practice, to televisions, to dinners on trays and sticky orange squash with fizzing vitamin supplements. Overhead, lights flickered to life, the voices faded out to the sound of rustling leaves and the icy wind. She liked it better this way. No hushed 'Are you all right, dear?' or 'I heard they're calling in special ed people, you know, 'cause she's ... you know'. No more whispers, or weird chattering, or questions she didn't care for, or about. Just silence, and the increasingly noisy skittering of pointed little legs across pavement, bark and flesh.

Something squelched; a soft, liquid sound, like fingernails across your eyes. She traced darkening skies and red-brick houses, all lined with ink, and found a smattering of beetles, congregated. A keen gasp; slack-jawed interest. Her bookbag hit the floor as she crouched down low, tilting her head this way and that to better inspect the black mass swarming sticky red and inky black.

A crow, spread this way and that, like an angel that had crashed into the ground. Bits of white stuck out from amidst muddled feathers; its head angled unnaturally. Beetles crawled all over it, so closely together they resembled one large shifting beast with a thousand legs and iridescent armour wrapped around its squishy insides. Their legs ripped and tore; small pincers and jaws worked furiously to crack and carve and *chew*.

They were eating it.

Heat surged in her tummy, tickling like prodding fingers. Words tumbled through her head; incomprehensible streams of ink, and worlds, and wonders. The beetles rubbed together like cicada jaws and sang holy communion as she watched them, yearning. They ate it all up, writhing in the small puddle of deep brown blood left behind, and she kept watching until it was too dark to do so.

At home, she dodged her mother's 'you're so late!' and 'how was class?'

and ran upstairs before 'think about your homework!' It didn't matter; it wasn't real. Her heart was pounding in her chest, her throat, her fingertips – the yearning had only grown, and she threw herself down to the carpet, clawed out books and papers and pens. Her whole body trembled as they came, scurrying feverishly out of corners and crevices, rushing to her, at her. They swarmed around her, over her, onto her; spilled forth from underneath her soles and behind her ears and covered every inch of her goosebumped skin.

She welcomed them, hungrily. They climbed into her mouth and slid down her throat, crusted underneath her fingernails and filled her chest with peals of laughter and delight. Filled her tummy with ink.

The vomit came easy, tar leaking from her mouth and spilling forth amidst her guts. Ink and paper, trembling fingers and sweat-stained beetles crawling through words and bile, punctuated with specks of darkness. She wasn't scared. Her thin body shook with excitement, with gravitas, with ecstasy. Teeth crunched on shattered shells; fingers ripped and tore and dug. A fevered shiver, a forceful birthing. A beginning, and an end.

When her mother called her down for dinner, no answer came. A few calls later, she headed up the stairs. But she found nothing in the little girl's room but a pile of papers and books, covered in ink and a scattering of dark, odd-looking beetles.

## *To Detangle and Relax My Night Hair*

*(A complete elegant solution for Lasting and Durable Tresses. Professionals only should carry out instructions listed below. Instructions are also provided overleaf in British English, French, Portuguese, Italian, Spanish, Belgian French. Straightening has never been easier, and leaves hair 4 times stronger for protection against breakage.)*

It reads: Do not lose the gold pin
      Balanced on the edge of your bed sheets;
It will be used to interlock your cornrows
Tightly into your braided spine
      I am adamant about my ownership of
What grows out of me; the outpour of my hair
      So real that it coils around me
Closer than impure thoughts
        Textured with lineage
Every predestined fibre of my life
          An echo
I dream, in this blackened room, a wet illusion of all
My indecisions. I spray bottle mist misst missst and yet
The dream refuses to end.
My grander optics propose only girls with no idea of who they want to be.

I reach – feeling between scissors and crepe paper
For instructions on how to relax.
The hair comb in my central
cord does not turn around all the way,
But roughens my hands all the same.

And my braid beads burn at the touch:
plastic and small and bright
'Do not get in your own way child'
'Your reflection is not the truth'

The night sits in the corner
Where the TV blue does not reach:
'Not every thought in your head is
What you deserve'

Around the needs of the infinite
4C coils,
My fingers and
I have broken all instructions
In hair maintenance.
In a way that will make
White women notice.
And will make my mother
Ask me to repeat after her:
That she braided me better than this;
      And all I can do is hold the crochet needle out and
      breathe
That her wisdom is necessary for life
      And there is no clear regulator for my Beautiful Beginnings®
That she knows the exact shape of my everything
because it first grew out of her
      And there is no clear separation of what regulates my
This time and the next and the next           breathing
      Our hair does not go away
Even when you put your lips together and blow
      There is a clear separation of pain in glory, unless it comes
      from certain bodies.
So I apply the dream-catching-no-lye-texturiser.
I hide behind the explanation
That I slipped into the chemicals of night as reflex.

Oh to know what this African head is growing!
Oh to know what I inherited and what is mine.
Of course, I am expansive and soft.
Of course, I am all this hair.
And a cold metal tooth comb
And also gleaming in Shea
And also golden.
It must be true
That if I stopped dying one day        all these petite split end deaths
It could all be spun into gold.
So real is the temporary balance
Of knowing what to do –

       What to detangle another's fingers out of –

    Of when to turn the mirror off –

       Of knowing what protective style to employ.

    Of knowing who to be for forty-two days.

       Of knowing who I will be

            at night.

That is when your hair is done.
The providence of an elastic band
holds the tiny bones in your wrists together.

                And you do not
                want to lose them.

# MARSHEA MAKOSA

*Champagne in Hand at a House Party*

Yet you and I agree this cannot continue,
This plod of dark horse shoes.

You are grounded in black heels.
There is a popular song imitating more classic feels,

So dance through the glittered bodies of chance,
Until someone catches your elbow to say:

> "Tell me what negroes know about how hard it
> is to be one anyway... no no listen, I heard...
> you must know, listen to be the ones leading the
> maladies of blackness that must..."

And this dead conversation you thought you'd buried brays, so
In the back of your mind, unseen, you become a noose wanderer,

Rope carrier, leading beaten horse conversations.
You taste the chomp of a trapped inter-dimension,

Leading over-worked horses from hills to shoreline,
To drink water from clear planes of Existence,

Every CPT. The reaper of the circumstance,
Counts his big gold coins; the governor of this one horse-town is time.

Technically this is not an ocean-splitting circumstance
But a *Happy New Year* tear
On your dressing gown, unseen.

Enjoy the conversations, the shotgunners believe
That every epoch from the earth is touchable.

That the names of victims are touchable, galloping clean in their mouths,
Curiosity wants to beat the horse of your ancestral pain, for you.

The shame of self-preservation will get you stuck in the mud, close
By someone says something behind a pale delicate hand,

And there, desperate again, lie more dead horses,
News cycle forces corpses out into the party, you cradle long horse faces,

> "'Equi donati dentes non inspicuintur'
> Don't look a black woman in the mouth
> My gums are black and everyone keeps reaching for my lips.
> To check for something? You good? You sure?
> You misunderstanding my role here; I am the gift. I'm the gift.
> My blackness threatens my life only when you speak on behalf of it."

Watch out for the falling dirt that smothered their slumber,
When the great ghoulish equines unfurl.

Held between you and I
Is the stretch between the grave and the universe's puddle.

The blue unhappy water
Suits you every time.

The broken window quality of dead horses, that wink with black tragedy.
You and I see how happy they were to have this discourse, drinks undrunk.

You and I see how handsome everyone is at this shoreline.
A tail swishes in your mind – their good intentions beat the air.

# SAOIRSE IBARGÜEN

*Forward* · Memoir

In darkness, I begin to climb the mountain. Shrouded in my tent for months, hiding from the nights that come after long days of aching legs, I've hardly seen the moon all year. But now it shines through the forest, allowing me to turn off my headlamp as I climb higher. I'm reminded that nighttime on this planet means a sky full of stars, and think I should have hiked by their light more often. But there is no point in looking back now.

Because I only need enough food for this final climb, my pack is lighter than it's been all year. But this mountain did not earn its respect and reverence by being easy, and the path grows steeper, as if the trail builders couldn't stand to prolong the glory any longer. As my body warms with the effort, I peel off layers of clothing and stuff them in my pack. But when I reach the tree line, moving beyond the forest and into the sky, the weather turns. The view hasn't changed, but I feel the shift like an animal feels the presence of its hunter. I collapse my poles and attach them to my pack. I'll need my hands now, and I'll need to hurry.

I'm in that blue hour just before sunrise, that limbo when the sky's blackness bleeds away and inky night changes eagerly, but with control, into brilliant day. My frozen hands almost slip as I pull myself up boulder after boulder, my body stretching to reach handholds that don't exist. For the last, and what seems like the thousandth time, I wish I was taller, that my limbs could reach safe places so I wouldn't always dangle over the nothingness, clinging to slick rock faces like a barnacle in a vast ocean, afraid to be swept away into the unknown depths. I can't be sure if adrenaline can carry me the rest of the way up, but I have no choice but to put my trust in the mountain, not knowing if I'll be making the return journey.

The wind picks up; no more quiet night now. I stand on a stable ledge, legs trembling like a newborn deer's, and turn around, pulling cold air into my lungs as my jaw drops at the sight: all of Maine, perhaps all of the world, glowing in the soft orange light of a late September morning.

I can only look for so long. The storm is coming, and I'm still two grueling vertical miles from the summit of Mount Katahdin, from the end of the Appalachian Trail. The weather was meant to be clear, but one thing I should've learned by now is that forecasts mean nothing, no one can see the future, and all I can ever do is keep pressing on, keep walking no matter what comes from the sky.

I pull myself up to the Gateway, the end of the most difficult part of the climb and the beginning of the Tablelands, a rock-strewn victory walk to the summit. But I can't taste the victory yet. I can no longer see the path to the end of this journey I've been on for six months.

With a howl almost too quiet for what it signifies, a sudden rush of clouds rolls in and entirely shrouds the mountain, closing me in, mercilessly erasing the panoramic views of Maine's jagged mountains and vast lakes. It all vanishes, all those miles I've hiked, all that land I wanted to look at from the very top. Now there is nothing but the mist, my boots, and my eyes straining to see ten feet in front of me.

I fight the urge to fall to my hands and knees and crawl the rest of the way. Though I'm bracing myself with all my strength, the wind is so strong that I imagine every time I lift a boot, I might be picked up and blown away. Could my body float back to Georgia and the beginning of the trail? Or would it go all the way to my home in Florida? I'm not sure where home is anymore.

I keep fighting, looking ahead, but thinking back, back to the early days of my hike, to North Carolina, when the weather was cold, but nothing like this. I remember the conversation I had with a German woman, one of many people I would meet from around the world, all drawn by the siren song of the longest footpath on Earth. The woman's trail name was Brick. Almost everyone who thru-hikes the Appalachian Trail acquires a trail name, gifted to them by other hikers, by themselves, by the journey. Mine is Story. Sitting with Brick in a hostel owned by a man named Zen, I both loved and felt baffled by this world of people walking, running away, using assumed names, banishing their "real" lives. I ran my hands over the leather cover of a decades old trail guide.

"It's strange, isn't it?" said Brick. "Just walking in one direction. Usually you walk for a bit and then turn around, go back to your car or something. But out here, you never look back." I didn't know what to say then; I just sat with her words. I couldn't know about any of the things I was hiking toward.

I couldn't foresee the spider that would find its way into my bra and bite me, the bite that would turn into a wound, the doctor who would dig at it with a scalpel while I sobbed in a church parking lot, surrounded by other injured hikers whose health and comfort were always at the mercy of strangers and volunteers. I couldn't have known that I would reach the halfway point and spend two hours forcing my way through half a gallon of chocolate ice cream, in order to uphold a longstanding trail tradition and prove my worth. I couldn't yet understand that all of the hardest miles truly were ahead of me, but that everything else was ahead of me, too. The changing of the leaves in New Hampshire, the wild ponies in Virginia, the verdant forests in Vermont, everyone singing "Take Me Home, Country Roads" and dancing at the yearly hiker festival, the trail magic and all the trail angels who would provide it, in the form of warm pancakes and fresh fruit and toilet paper out of the backs of their trucks on the side of the road somewhere in the mountains. All of these things were yet to come.

"Out here, you never look back," Brick said.

For 185 days, I have not looked back. I have trudged up mountains, brown with dead leaves and deep mud. I have bounded down hills, green and vibrant in their summer glory. I have faced black bears and rattlesnakes, looked in their shining eyes and kept on walking. I have suffered hard falls and sickness, felt my skin slick with sweat and my muscles seized from exertion. I have climbed mountains from dawn until dusk every day for half a year. I've carried my life on my back and slept in the woods. I've walked 2,190.9 miles. I've traveled all the way from Georgia to Maine on my feet.

Even at the end, I barely have an answer to give people when they ask why I'm doing this. I'm doing it for the little girl who knew she was meant to hike even though she was born in a swamp and had only the flattest pavement to walk on. I'm doing it because it was that little girl's biggest dream and I could never rest until I put my hands on that sign at the end of all those miles. For her, and for the me that she grew into, I keep heading north.

On this last push to the summit, I think of my first day, on top of Springer Mountain in Georgia, questioning whether I could really do this. I think of the panic attack in my tent, my breath coming in short gasps as the wind whipped around me and I felt like a broken rowboat on a wild sea. Now I've almost done it, and the summit fever takes me.

I may not be able to see anything through the clouds, but I know which direction to move in: forward. My feet scramble, my arms reach out to prevent a fall this close to the end. I stumble over wet rocks with abandon, knowing what's so close now, maybe just a few feet away. Blinded with melting frost dripping from my hat and my braids whipping across my eyes, I squint and can finally make out a wooden sign, desolate, alone on top of the world, waiting for me to touch it after years of dreaming. I know what it says without reading it. I rush forward into the mist.

# ALICE ROGERS

*Comet Viscara*

"I was there at the start of all things," he says, voice low in the midnight black. I hum, the hand of the firelight the only thing making him more than a smudge of black on black, and pull the tie from the end of his long braid.

"Is that so?"

"I breathed the first breath."

"Ate the first chicken, huh?"

I comb my fingers through his hair, working the strands from their tight braid. Long and so black that it swallows the firelight, so thick that it's still damp from our morning wash. Now the night breeze sweeps over us and the fire dips its brow at its passing, and he shifts, tucks his kerchief into the collar of his jacket.

"There were no chickens at the start of things, Samson." There's a shadow of a smile in his voice.

I chuckle. "No good eatin', shit." I ease the top of his braid free and scratch my fingernails at his scalp, smiling at his groan. "Good?"

"Sore." He grunts. "No, keep going."

"Keep tellin' me your stories and I will."

"It ain't a story, Sam, it's—"

Gently, I murmur, "Memory, I know," and wait a beat, let the silence make itself known. "Just tell me."

The absolute silence of the valley needs a voice to cover it up. The fire ain't enough. The soft sounds of breathing and shifting from our horses ain't, either. All those natural sounds just ease into each other, ease into the whole damn orchestra of the world until you feel like you're a part of it too. No, you need something to cut through it, something to pierce it, something to remind you that things exist outside of our circle of firelight.

The things we want to think about existing. Family, home, love. I care less about the coyotes wanting a mouthful of my ass.

We're sheltered for the night in the belly of the valley, the mountains on either side dark and indistinct watchers. Been following the river for four days, moving through the gorge on horseback along the snake-like twists and turns. I shot and killed a pair of rabbits during the day, and he skinned and gutted them just before nightfall. And here we are now. Bellies full, warmed by the fire, the sky vast and starry above our heads.

"I saw a burning rock in the sky one night," he says, head tilted back into my hands. From what I can see of him by the firelight, his eyes are closed, that sweet and vacant expression of someone who believes they're unwatched. I scratch through the still-damp hair that flows out over his shoulders, wavy from his braid, from being tied up dripping. This morning we led the horses into the river; cooled them down and then ourselves. I think of the shine of sunlight on the water, the warmth of the sun on the crown of my wet head.

"What did it mean?" I ask.

"The end of all things." He shifts, hand going to his breast pocket, to his tobacco. "A god's anger."

He rolls a cigarette. I wait, listening to the sounds of the night. The babble of the river, the rush of wind in the trees. He smells like leather and sweat, but when I lean in close and put my nose to the crown of his head, I can smell him beyond. Crook of the elbow smell, hollow of the throat. Warm skin and salt.

The story isn't finished. It's one I've heard before and will doubtless hear again. Each time is a little different but it all smooths out into the same thing, like the meat around it can change but the skeleton ain't got the same privilege.

"I was farmin' maize up in Iowa," he says, finally, drawing on his cigarette. That's part of the skeleton, that detail. One of the things that don't change. "Saw it before anybody else."

It was his daddy who'd seen it, in 1901; before he and I would've been allowed to drink in the same saloon. I make a grab for his cigarette, which he surrenders easily.

"And I was scared. Scared because I ain't seen nothin' like that before in any of my lives, but I'd heard enough stories to know to be scared. I was sure it'd kill me, whether it'd be right then when I was stuck fast to the ground in my fear, or whether it'd be in whatever sickness was going to fall after it."

I take a drag from my stolen cigarette, listening. The wind brings with it the smell of the valley, of dark earth and fresh grass, the green, organic smell of the river. But I ain't here. I'm there; Iowa, the smell of maize in my nose, and a great red star in the sky burning spots into my eyes.

"Like a little sun. Like a star had fallen loose from the sky," he adds.

"Where did it go?"

"It looped around the world and it'll come back for us one day." His voice is steady, deliberate. I pass him back his cigarette, slip my arm around his chest and pull him to mine. Just like the cigarette, he goes easy. "We bathed ourselves in mud to escape it the first time, when it scorched the earth bare."

"Did you get sick?"

"I died four years later, on horseback."

We're both silent for a time. My heart thumps away against his back, a dim reminder of my one life. Feels like nothing next to his. I inch my fingers in between the buttons of his jacket, through to that warm space between the sheepskin and the flannel of his shirt. His heart pounds against my palm.

"'S the only way to go," I murmur finally, and he hums in agreement. I cast my eyes up, trying to work out just what and how I'd feel if I saw the same sight. A star wiggled loose from the gum of the sky. Is it the sort of thing you wish on? "Where d'you keep your stories?"

The glowing tip of his cigarette makes a path from knee to temple. "Here," and then his hand pats over mine, warm inside his coat. "Here. And I keep 'em in my family."

"They were all there at the start'a things too, huh?"

He laughs at that, twisting in my hold to grin at me. Firelight in his black eyes. "Yeah, they were there too."

"Was I?"

His eyes crinkle. "Well, do you remember it?"

I can see where this is going. "I don't."

He nods and sinks back against my chest, the light of the flames flickering gently on his profile. "Then that settles that."

Out here in the country at night, it feels like we could be the only people left in the world. Just us, our circle of firelight, my mare and his proud-cut gelding. I think I'd like that; just the two of us. Nobody to act like anyone other than ourselves around, no one for him to avert his eyes from. Just me and him and his stories, and our fruitless little search for gold along this vein of a river. Earlier in the day I watched him stand knee-deep in the river, pan in his hands and his face all twisted up with focus. *Four*, he said. *Nothin' but specks.* Brought me the pan to inspect the gold inside.

"I think it got cleared out years ago," he's saying, sounding drowsy, leaning heavier against me now. "Our gold rush is a little too late."

Funny how he can track the tides of my thoughts like that.

"We'll go all the way along to California," I reply, though I care less about the gold. Miles in his company, heaven come early. "Find you somethin' pretty to put in your hair."

He laughs at that. "Samson, I'll hold you to that." Then he leans forward, and I let him move out of the circle of my arms even though I hate to do it. My hands go to his hair, go to the tangled little knot he always gets at the nape of his neck.

"This ain't easin' out for nobody," I murmur, moving with him as he reaches to toss some more kindling on the fire. It takes it hungrily, sparks drifting up toward the sky as the wood settles and pops in the flames. I have a comb in my saddlebag but I don't like hurting him; like working the tangle loose for as long as it needs to take.

"We got time," he says, and I kiss his temple just to smell his hair again. Past the sweat, past the dirt, that human smell.

I say, "Tell me another story," and listen to his voice cut clear through the night, thinking of the comet with its tail wrapped around the world.

LAUREN N. THURMAN

*History*

She got the first one when she was ten. It's near her right armpit, a purplish splotch on the creamy underside of her arm. Emma was walking home from school, in her sprawled suburban neighborhood of split-levels and parched lawns, when she turned onto the third street from her house and a flurry of motion caught her eye. A man was sitting halfway out the driver's seat of his car with his pants pulled over his knees and his hand moving up and down between his legs like he was trying to get ketchup out of a bottle. He was smiling at her.

Emma's face was hot. She felt ashamed, though she wasn't sure why, and she hurried up the street and around the corner. She turned back once to check if he was still looking at her but all she could see was his open car door. She didn't tell her parents—it would have made her feel even more ashamed, to talk about it—and the next morning she noticed the splotch. When her mom grabbed her arm and asked, "Honey, what's this?" Emma said it was just a bruise from the monkey bars and from then on she wore longer sleeves.

The spot got a little bigger when she was seventeen. She stepped out of a friend's car on a hot summer day and the memory of another man in another car came back to her, sharp and sudden. She breathed through her teeth as she understood more fully what had happened, what she had been made part of, and the splotch grew to the size of a small child's hand. But by then it wasn't her only one. She got the second when she was thirteen and a guy pinched her ass at the mall—on a dare, she heard. The spot showed up right where his index finger had really dug in. She thought it was a bruise, but it just never went away. When, in junior year, a senior boy sent a group of her friends a picture of his genitals, a splotch bloomed on the back of her knee.

"You mean you don't get stuff like this, after guys do things like that?" she asked her friend Corinne the next day. Emma had thought they would be comparing splotches, but Corinne had only stared at her.

"That's crazy, dude. I've never seen anything like that."

"Like my spots or like... that?" Emma nodded meaningfully toward the blank screen of her phone, which was heavy and potent with the new threat of things it could show them.

"Like *those*," Corinne said, gesturing to the parts of Emma's body where she had just shown off her marks. "You get them any time something like this happens?"

Emma nodded. "Pretty much, yeah."

"Weird. I can't believe you don't have more."

The biggest one stretches across her lower abdomen. It looks like an upside-down map of Africa, with everything north of the Sahara dipping below her underwear. This is what she can remember: she woke up on a stranger's couch after a party in college, walked home with her head blasted to bits, and found the new splotch when she undressed to take a shower. She freaked out and went to urgent care, where she told them she needed a rape kit.

"Do you wish to report the incident to the authorities at this time?" the nurse asked her.

"I don't know who it was," Emma said. "I don't remember anything from last night." She felt like crying.

"Then how do you know you were raped?"

Emma explained the splotches. She lifted her arm and told the nurse about the guy jacking off in his car. She pointed to her ass and to the back of her knee and said that she got a new one each time something like this happened.

"That seems a little extreme," the nurse said. "Are you sure you're not just overreacting?"

She tried scrubbing, scraping, bleaching. Serums and cleansers and toners and peels. Her acne scars faded, but the splotches stayed bright and vivid as ever—and every so often a new one appeared. She avoided tank tops, shorts, thin fabrics. For a while she couldn't face the sharp edges of the world at all; she avoided bars and off-peak public transit and certain aisles of the grocery store. The marks were memories, too, and it was about living with them just as much as it was about looking at them.

Some of her close friends told her to show them off, like they were evidence, like her body was some kind of a living rebuke. Her mother gently suggested that she wear more jewel tones, to avoid clashing. Once, Emma psyched herself up enough to wear a pencil skirt to work. She spent the whole day tense, waiting for someone to ask, "What's on the back of your leg?" But nobody did. Her friend Chloe sent an email after lunch that said, "Girl, you are ROCKING that look. You're so strong and I'm proud of you."

When Chloe invited her down to the Outer Banks for a long weekend at her family's beach house, Emma wanted to say no. She pictured herself in a swimsuit, her splotches bared to the world, and cringed. But Chloe worked on her, promising to lend a sundress and make endless blended drinks, until Emma relented. Until she was even a little excited to feel the sand between her toes.

That was where she met Andrew. She blushed when they met, and she blushed when he set up a beach chair next to hers, and her eyes followed him wherever he moved. On her second day there, spurred by a little day-drinking and by the heavy, comforting heat of the ocean air, Emma took off her borrowed dress and waded into the water with Chloe. She was wearing an old bikini, the only swimsuit she owned, and the mark on her stomach was a loud fuchsia dipping in and out of the water. She lay back and let the waves hold her, and when she closed her eyes she found that she could breathe easily. She didn't feel horribly visible; she was just a part of the ocean's surface. Emma spread her arms wide so that the armpit splotch winked up at the sky. The sun was warm on her eyelids and she tasted salt on her lips. When she came back onto the sand, she glanced over at Andrew to look for any signs of change in his eyes, in the set of his shoulders. But he only smiled at her and asked if she wanted his towel; it was dry.

They exchanged numbers. The next week he drove four hours up to D.C. to see her, and she blushed at this too. When she hungrily invited him home, she didn't worry about showing him the splotches because he had already seen them back on the beach. She savored the ease of it. His hands ran over the marked parts of her body like they weren't even there, like they were just skin.

When he slid his boxers off, a flash of color caught her eye. There. On his left hip. The same pinkish-purple as hers, like the flesh of a ripe plum.

"Oh my god," she said.

Emma sat up and held her hands up above his body, suddenly afraid to touch. To break. She searched his face, hoping it would tell her the right thing to say. She felt like crying.

He reached for her hands and set them softly onto the mattress, close to the heat of his chest. His thumb roved across her knuckles. "We can talk about it if you want," he said. "But we don't have to. I don't know about you, but it's such a relief not to have to talk about it."

Emma lay back down. She wrapped her arm around his torso and squeezed, as gently as she knew how.

SKYE WILSON

*The Farrier's Daughter*

Two hundred years ago, my blood
picked up a hammer.
The blows have formed my bones:
I am seventeen hands tall,
thirteen to the withers, and every day
I weave my hair into a tail.

Once a length of steel is made
white-hot and hammered into shape
it is plunged in cold water, hardens,
becomes strong again. Last year
I almost drowned, but I was forged
in fire – I am my flame.

Mounted on a wall the right way up,
a horseshoe forms a bowl; holds luck
for your home. Farriers hammer
them, heels down, over our doors.
I am nothing now, although I will be:
I don't gather luck, I make my own.

## SKYE WILSON

*the girls are laughing in the gym*

striding in, an army, matching
shorts and sports bras, bruises blooming
on thick thighs, high ponytails fly
from side to side as we strut,
scope the weights room, carve out our
corner with explosive snorts of laughter, teeth
glinting white in fluorescent mouths
wide enough to swallow shame, shoulders
squared against men who mean to shrink us
but always smiling at other women.
we invite them, cackling, into our coven
share our bottles of protein potion,
protect each other, learn to look after
ourselves, feel our fibres tear, rebuild, renew.

## SKYE WILSON

*Prayer*

May every aspect of your body belong to you alone.

May you remain unbroken, emanate warmth,
have your blazing heart held by those who know it best.
May every mouthful be just food: no struggle,
no victory, nothing
but sustenance, bliss and togetherness.

May you find joy in dancing or rugby; lipsticked
mouths or stubbled cheeks; the smell
of new countries, the dew in highland glens.
May you never question the core
of who you are – may no one ever shake it.
Let me help you hold it steady.
May your world begin again with each fresh
blush of sunrise. May you change the earth
with every gentle breath
before the twilight comes.

*Jack of Hearts*

We escaped the lashing rain
to find a pint and a game of cards.
You betrayed your brother with a laugh:
*no one's sadder than me, Dave,*
but always slipped your niece the card I needed.

*Blind positivity in all things:*
they caught it early.

You taught me card tricks, introduced me
to my new favourite chocolate;
spent the summer cycling for fruit,
spreading brie too thick on fresh bread.

*Blind positivity in all things:*
you were in remission
when your son dropped out of uni.
You told him: *better things will come.*

A packet of crisps and a pint,
sun gleaming on your glass and blinding
legs sprawled from the ugliest shorts
I've ever seen. Lounging on the bench,
you looked out to the loch, eyes half closed.

*Blind positivity in all things:*
you bet on West Brom every week,
and rarely won. Their stripy scarves
were all around the funeral
(no black allowed)
then we went back to yours,
had a pint, played some cards.

CHENSHUO WANG

*Pickles*

'On the 14th of November, 1959, the last week of autumn, Li, a chain-smoker, tilled his garden and got rid of his withered plants, five dead plants out, one finished cigarette. The night was cloudy and full of cold damp air, as he sowed the seeds of Chinese jasmine into his deserted garden in darkness.

'A week later, the day was crisp and cloudless. A tranquil and green bud of a no-name plant sprouted from the brown and dead stump beside the fence, and the odour of wet dirt permeated Li's garden. The blue river, which had once been bustling and made the pebbles clink together, was running slowly around his house, and the surfaces of the pebbles were exposed to the dry sunlight. While the soft breeze quivered the red flag jutting from the roof, Li carried half a bucket of water back from the river bank, with a cigarette held in his mouth.

'On the 24th of November, a group of trucks loaded with grain passed by his house, where a gingko tree stood, looking like a mass of golden fog. The dust rising from the wheels went through the tree, powdered it and coloured it dirt brown. Li, sitting on the dead stump and smoking, noticed many people running, chasing the trucks and passing by him. Some of them were exhausted and sat on the ground. Those less exhausted staggered back to the quiet gingko tree. Li put his cigarette out and slipped the rest of it into his pocket. When he stood up, ready to escape from them, he found some people were eating the tender twigs of his tree.

'At midnight of the same day, the moon was misty. A haze drifted over and transiently veiled the moon, and the moonlight floated like a deep blue pool. The jasmines sprouted silently, oozing a scent of sweetness and satiety.

'Next morning, all of the sprouts disappeared. Oddly, those people were refreshed. They turned up again and continued to chase the new trucks that came. Staring at his forlorn garden, Li didn't even sigh. He turned back and walked into his wretched house. He spoke to his son and wife, "We have neither money nor seed now. We have to move and visit my second brother. He'll help us." Then he told them to go off first and that he would catch them up later. That night before they left, with their son sleeping on the wife's knees, she whispered to Li, "The food... There's not enough food left for us three. If I can't make it," the wife was caressing her son, "you must take care of our son." Her voice was fainter than the groan of a dying cricket outside the draughty window. Li nodded, taking out a box of matches and lighting up a handmade cigarette. He smoked thirteen in total, one after another, until the matches ran out. The wife could only see his back silhouette trembling as the candlelight ahead of him flickered. She gently fanned her son, dissipating the smoke drifting to him.

'Next morning, the wife departed with her son. When they arrived at the appointed place, they sat down waiting for Li until sunset. The wife felt something was wrong and rushing back to their house in great haste, found her husband had hanged himself and was facing his lifeless garden which had once been ablaze with colourful flowers thriving in...'

'Thank you for sharing. It's amazing.'

'Agreed. That's heartbreaking. What did they eat when they were heading to ...' My classmate looks down at the manuscript to check the exact word. I know having too many children, like more than three, is not so common in the UK. '... second brother's home?'

I hesitate, for I don't like saying too much about my homeland. 'Wo tou. Some kind of ... bread, I think?' I look through the window at those bare and sharp treetops of no-name trees, because I only know one type of tree species, the gingko tree. 'But you can imagine it as the dark bread for the poorest in Chinese version. And pickles.' I just associate them with those yellow pickled cucumbers in glass jars. I continue, 'They also took pickles, because pickles hardly go off. And they're salty, adding some flavour to tasteless wo tou.' I'm salivating. The flavour of sour and salty comes back to my tongue. I'm starving.

My mind sometimes drifts. I confess this is absolutely disrespectful to my classmates' fabulous work, but I'm so hungry and can't help thinking of the foods from my land.

After the class, one of my classmates asks me if I've tried writing historical novels before. I answer no. This is the first time and it's based on the Great Chinese Famine. What I don't tell him is that this is not a historical novel; actually, it's a memoir. The protagonist is my grandfather's father. We must know, storytelling is tricky. No one knows if it is real or not other than the author. Sometimes I deliberately conceal the truth. I'm just worried I'll receive more 'kindness' and 'sympathies' than I can take.

As I leave the campus, waiting at a bus stop, there is an Asian couple in the queue in front of me. They get into the bus and talk to the driver for a long time. The biting coldness in Edinburgh has ruined my patience. I stamp my feet and go forward, finding out they barely know how to speak English. The driver tries to communicate with them at a very slow talking speed. My movement rattles the couple. They take out their phones and, with the help of the translator, they finally get it. When the driver notices me, he talks like the sloth named Flash in *Zootopia* – 'WHERE ARE YOU GOING?' – a simple sentence with huge intervals between each syllable. 'Princes Street,' I tell him. While he is gesturing, probably trying to explain how to pay the ticket, I tap my card and go quickly to the upper deck.

I know lots of people here are kind and friendly, but I think outlanders, at least some of us, have too much trouble blending in, as if we were an ink droplet in a glass of water, and that personally stings my heart. The bus lurches and jolts me; it saunters like a lost cub along the hilly cobbled road, up to the antique and winding Grassmarket road and down to the modern and flat Princes Street.

When I arrive, I have to confront the same embarrassment that I had in China. The enormous crowd. It's very hard to maintain your sense of direction and personal will when you have to jump into the rapid stream of passers-by. I do as I did before, standing out in the crowd. It's hard to believe such a place saturated with lots of people does exist outside of Asia. I see an old man holding a cigarette, with yellowed nails on his index and middle fingers, walk slowly in the crowd. A crimson poppy is pinned on his coat. And a young couple, holding shopping bags with a big logo on them, walk behind the old man. A small flock of seagulls is hovering over the crowd. The huge shadows of their wings cover the shop windows, and two or three kids are observing the shadows and are guessing where they are coming from.

I enter the store. All I search for is the main ingredient of a Chinese-style pickle. If I directly translate the name of it, it will be *Redness in the Snow*. Embarrassingly, I don't know its English name. I sneak a look at the customers, making sure no one will notice me. Then I take out my phone and open the dictionary app. Well, the result is pretty accurate at least – the *brassica juncea*. But it seems that this is not a common name known by customers. I try to seek help, and find a staff member who is talking with an old lady. I walk towards them and stop by a shelf about twelve feet away from them. I wait, but their talking is seemingly endless.

When I'm about to leave, I find there is a jar of pickles standing silently on the shelf. I buy it and take it home. There is really nothing to say about it. It starts with a crunchy texture, then comes the sour and salty flavour, and it ends in crunchier bites and the juicy pulp spreading out. After a pickle goes into my stomach, I find a very familiar taste lingering on my tongue, as if a warm redness is reviving in the cold snow. Three years and 83 days – this is how long I've been living in this foreign land, where the clouds are drifting much faster than those in my hometown; and where the dry east wind can never reach.

## L. K. KRAUS

*Sherwood*

We're in the schoolyard and he's pretending to hump me from behind. It's a joke. It's funny. Hilarious. Only that I feel embarrassed; I don't want his greasy sweat and too-much-deodorant on me. This is so humiliating; it's not funny at all. I don't understand why everybody seems to think it is. Do they really? Or do they just laugh along with him because everything else would require effort, force them to reveal what they're thinking, who they are – to confront him, make him uncomfortable? Why is his comfort more important than mine? He is the one doing something he could stop. I try to get away, but he tightens his grip.

This is ridiculous. I'm strong, I can easily throw him off. I put up more of a fight now, but he has an advantage because he was already holding me so tightly when I started struggling. I can feel his sweaty hands staining my t-shirt. I cry out furiously. An animal cry; no words, just desperation. Fear and disgust are prickling throughout my body. I strain against his sticky arms, damp chest. A few people look in our direction, concern on their faces at first, but it turns into grins and then they laugh again. They must have looked at him, and I guess he smiled his usual self-assured smile.

Veronica and Maisy are standing a little further away, observing the group, observing me. Why aren't they coming over? They're my friends! Veronica's gaze meets mine, she holds it for a while, then turns demonstratively and starts chatting to Maisy. I'm panicking now – I can feel my legs turning to water and my palms sweat. I want to scratch and tear, but he's holding my arms. How can they still not get it? Why is nobody doing anything? I force myself to clear my head enough to shout, 'No! No, I don't want this! Get off me! Leave me alone! No!'

•

'Why did you have to make such a fuss?' Veronica asks me later.

One of the teachers had come to my rescue eventually, ordering Craig to let go of me, but not saying anything more about it. Veronica and Maisy ignored me when I started walking towards them, so I turned and hid in the toilets instead until it was time to go back to class.

'Seriously. You don't do that. It's just a bit of fun. You smile and say something funny. They stop a lot quicker when they can't make you angry.'

'You will never get a boyfriend if you're like that,' Maisy adds.

It all started a couple of weeks ago, when they didn't want to go to the forest. Like every day, we had switched our walkie-talkies to channel five after school.

'We can't come today. We're watching *The Tribe* – the next episode is on soon.'

I heard somebody giggling in the background. Was that Veronica?

'Friar Tuck, is Will Scarlet with you?' They would have told me if they were meeting up, wouldn't they?

'This is Will Scarlet, yes, I'm here. We've got to go. Our series is starting.'

What was this series? Since when did they watch TV? *We* didn't watch TV. Did we still have a we? What about our headquarters? We'd found the perfect spot to build a new one after our cosy treehouse got destroyed. This time, nobody would find it. I realised I was just staring at the walkie-talkie, switched it off and walked over to the window. I had been excited to go out, but now it looked cold, uninviting. I could have just stayed in and read, but we really had to finish the hut. Our club book was at Veronica's – her brother could find it!

I normally ran across the terrace, jumped off and skipped along the path, though I might have stopped to feel the hazel catkins, picking a handful and stripping them of the little crumbly bits, leaving a trail behind me, thinking of fairy tales. I didn't run that day. It was autumn, so there were no catkins either, just hints of smoke from the first coal fires when I breathed in.

I felt better as soon as I reached the forest, with its smell of pine sap in the fresh almost-winter air and the light filtering through the branches. I spotted a cluster of mushrooms that hadn't been there before and crouched down to feel the cool, silky-smooth caps before I carried on, faster now, then starting to run. I stopped before I turned the corner where the fenced-off area started. I had to look inconspicuous, just in case somebody was walking their dog. Our hut was in a regrowth area of the forest – nobody was allowed to go in there. We'd put a lot of effort into building a path that wouldn't be visible from the outside even if we walked it often, using the pine-needle carpet under small trees, old deer paths, and sections of tunnel we'd built in the ferns.

The path was empty, so I ran to the edge of the fence as quickly as I could, put my hands on the rough top of the corner post, ignoring the splinters, and pulled myself up and over. Squatting low, I quickly covered the distance between the fence and the undergrowth. This was the easy part, because it went through a little copse of pines, I was able to walk upright, and the needly carpet wouldn't betray my footsteps.

On reaching the clearing where the hut would be, I started working right away. I made a whole wall from ferns and fallen branches, until heaviness crept from my arms and legs into my chest. I'd been working quickly, keeping myself from thinking, but now thoughts were unfurling from every corner of my mind. Why hadn't they wanted to come to the forest? What was this series they were watching, how did they know about it, and why was it more interesting than the new HQ for our Robin Hood Club? I sealed one last gap with moss, then I started walking back, careful not to bend the ferns.


On the weekend, they ran out of excuses and came into the forest with me, to see what I'd done. They were clumsy on the path, trampling the ferns, talking loudly and without code-names. *What are you doing?* I wanted to hiss, but something told me to keep my mouth shut. I could only hope that there wasn't anybody nearby to hear us.

We got to the hut, and they didn't even look at my wall at first. They were still talking about the series.

'Do you even want our club still?' I was the one asking, but I wasn't sure where the question came from. Suddenly, it felt like I'd been wanting to ask it for a long time, and somehow it was really scary to wait for the answer. Little John and Will Scarlet were inspecting the leaves at their feet.

'I'm relieved you asked.' They looked at each other. 'We don't, actually. It's super childish.'

They didn't even seem sorry; it was like they were trying to suppress laughs! This made it impossible for me to say I disagreed.

'Okay, then.' I took my knife out of my pocket. It was stuck under the whistle and the handkerchief. Rookie mistake! You should always have easy access to your knife. But maybe that didn't matter anymore? Having finally unfolded it, I slid the blade under the club bracelet on my wrist and pulled. The colourful cord fell to the ground. I forced myself not to look at it and held the knife out to Veronica and Maisy. They showed me their naked wrists. They'd already taken theirs off.

A little later, I found out what it had been all about. They'd decided they wanted to be proper girls – they were grown up now, and what we'd been doing was suddenly 'childish.' A lot of things were childish now, or immature. They said it wasn't my fault my parents didn't teach me girly things. They said we could still be friends, but only if I also wanted to be a proper girl and let them help me act like it. I would need to watch the series with them, so I could join their conversations. They took me shopping, and I bought two blouses. I started wearing my hair in a neat ponytail with a sparkly hairclip. They shushed me when I talked back to boys, they told me to smile at them instead. During breaks, they made me get coffee now, because hot chocolate was for babies, and it had too many calories. They put mascara and lipstick on me. I would wipe off most of the lipstick on my sleeve, but leave the mascara. This was how I looked when Craig started noticing me.

KATIE HAY

*and so they danced*

There was a Mountain once, a very young Mountain which pierced the Clouds with its jagged summit and scorned the Snows' feeble attempts to remain on its slopes. It was so tall none knew its peak but the Wind. The Wind loved to play in the Mountains, particularly with this young Mountain, because it seemed to the Wind that her Mountain knew very much about very little. It hid its curiosity in its yawning caves, and she enjoyed teasing pebbles from the solid stone.

Today began as did most winter days with her Mountain.

"How exhausted you must be from all your coming and going," said the Mountain to the freshly fallen Snows. "I am glad I am a Mountain. I don't have to worry about such things as disappearing and remaking myself. You are here now, but soon you will be nothing but memory."

Sparkling in the Sun, the Snows answered, "Ah, but we will return, as we always do."

"And I will be here, as I always am."

"You were not always here. Once, you swirled below the Earth you now gloat over. Your memory is not so great: you have forgotten what it is to be made and therefore cannot imagine yourself unmade."

The Mountain scoffed, "If I am to be unmade, it is to be so long from now that it may as well be never."

"Forever and a long time are not the same."

"You think yourself so wise. You rise and fall like the Sun, but this does not make you infinite."

"Oh how young the wisdom of crags!" laughed the Wind, wrapping herself around the Mountain's ridges. "Dear Mountain, the Snows move in seasons shorter but not lesser, and though they vanish from sight, they are no more absent than I appear to be. Your seasons are longer but no greater.

You forget that Mountains too rise and fall, and, like the Snows, one day I will lift your feet from the ground and we will dance."

"You know many things, Friend, but you do not know how Mountains work," said the Mountain. "Stone does not dance. It will fall apart."

"But you are a Mountain," the Wind whistled. "You are more than stone."

The Mountain shuddered, and the Snows cascaded down its slope in shimmering white sheets tossed into the air by the Wind's playful fingers. The Mountain refused to say anything more for millennia, because if tossings-about were what dancing looked like, the Mountain wanted nothing to do with it.

Despite the Mountain's reticence, the Wind visited often, bringing seeds and stories and songs. Slowly, the Mountain's steep stony skin grew into a smooth gentle slope, and scraggly Trees multiplied into dense Forests. Fed by the Snows and encouraged by the Wind, the Trees nestled into the Mountain, ever chattering in their many voices—crisp oranges, pliable greens, damp blues and browns—for they loved sharing stories.

The Trees one day grew weary of their Mountain's silence and rustled, "Awake, you Mountain! What keeps you so hushed?"

"Do not call me Mountain," the Mountain said, "for I am no more than a Hill now. I am melting as if I were no greater than the Snows."

The Trees shook and a few of their leaves joined their siblings on the floor. "The Snows are quite great! The Snows can rip us up by our roots as if we had never laid them. You *are* no greater than they."

"I was, once."

"Certainly, you were unbending and hard. That did not make you great. Consider your friend, the Wind. She cannot pierce our trunks, and our branches break her songs into howls, yet does this steal her strength?"

The Mountain quaked, "Of course not! She could snatch you from my skin just as the Snows."

"And yet rarely does she. Instead, she bends us. She teaches us to trust our roots even when our limbs stretch so high, the Clouds cover our feet. She reminds us of our strength, and this makes her great."

"The Wind is great indeed, but I am not like her. I once pierced the Clouds and now they forget my name, and, well they should, for it is no longer mine. I am being unwritten."

"Oh dear Mountain!" the Wind exclaimed, startling the Trees, for she had a habit of appearing unannounced. "You once thought so highly of yourself, and now you think too little. A Mountain's story is many. I have seen Mountains that quake and split like seeds, Mountains that dance as if they are made of water. I know Mountains of azure and cream, their ridges crested with running salmon; they burst from nothing and sink into inky soil with each evening and morning and hide during the day. These are no less, no more, Mountain than are you."

"But I am less of myself. Each year, more trees find home in my soil. Each day, you carry more of me to other Mountains. You reduce me to a Hill."

"My dear Mountain, you are less of what you were, but that does not mean you are less of who you are. Did you not hear the Trees? When the Sky bids them fly, you ground them. Do you not see the beauty of it? The Clouds know you anew, they find you in the Trees' canopies and in dust exposed. Your heart breathes in ways stone never allowed."

The Mountain kept its heart buried deep and wrapped in magma, as all Mountains' hearts should be. "I know that you are in the air, Friend, but I do not like the sound of being so naked."

The Wind laughed, tenderly stroking the Mountain with her hand. "Few do, dear Mountain. You are still young and it is a terrifying thing to be vulnerable. But when you are old, you will trust me as the Trees, and then we will dance."

This excited and troubled the Mountain, who, having no boulders to cleft, furrowed its shifting soil. The Trees wrestled with the Wind, their toes shuffling the Mountain's skin to their liking, and the Snows blanketed the ground, muffling the Mountain's voice. All the while, the Mountain brooded, convinced that to be Mountain and to be Dust were as different as life and death themselves, and only great fools believed one was as wonderful as the other.

•

Time out of mind passed, and the Snows fell, the Trees thickened, the Wind sang, and the Mountain whom the Wind loved and who loved the Wind, this Mountain grew. It grew until it became a low rolling plain of rich soil created by millennia of churning over by the Snows and the Trees. And though the Mountain changed, the Wind always visited as if no time had gone.

"My dear Mountain, you are so heavy today!" breathed the Wind as she gusted across the fields. "Have the Rains persuaded you to become stone again?"

"Do not speak to me, Wind, for I am no longer here."

The Wind swirled, "Well, if you are gone, whose voice do I hear? I do not think the Moles and Voles yet know my tongue."

"It is as you once said, so long ago. I have vanished and am no longer your Mountain."

"Dear Mountain, do not put words into my mouth. You are certainly my Mountain. Nowhere on Earth or in Sky do I find such melodrama as in you."

The Mountain leapt into the air, indignant. "I once sliced the Sky in two and trapped the Earth as my footstool! Now, I am scattered; I am so many pieces, I am nothing. How strong I was, dear Wind, and now I am too weak to keep your invisible hands from tossing me about."

"Water is no less itself when it fractures and only then do we see the colors it hides in its Rivers and Snows. Yes, you once rifted the Sky with your stony flesh. You tried to hide your heart even from me. Now you are fractured and your veins are unhidden."

The Mountain groaned. "I was a Mountain; now I am Dust."

"Before, you were thick and unyielding. Now, you have grown old and know what it is to both resist and be moved by others. You are today my Mountain."

"I dare not hope you speak truth."

"You must dare, my Mountain! When you were stone, I sang to you and you would not raise your feet for fear of falling apart. Now that you have fallen apart, raise your feet! Time has hidden you from yourself, but you are not gone. See, I can finally hold you."

The Wind lifted the Mountain into the Sky and threw it in a million directions, broken before the Sun. The Trees clapped as this Mountain who argued with the Snows tasted the Wind's embrace and together they knew what it was to dance.

*Changing Room*

She peels down her tights, slowly fattening the slippery roll of black nylon into one thick hoop around her ankles. A girl sitting on the opposite bench, already dressed in a skort binding slim, milky legs into one smooth ski slope, mimes shading the glare of a bright sun from her eyes as she watches the tights descend, squinting in disgust before doubling over into full-throated laughter.

Pale blue benches lining the walls hold a scatter of others, chattering. Judgement spreads like wildfire in the changing room, and, soon enough, they catch onto the fuss and turn towards her too. They stare as she pulls her gym shorts up underneath the protective veil of the uniform skirt, grazing the wiry spider legs sticking out from her calves. The girls tut, running their fingers over their shaven kneecaps.

Careful not to flash the spill of her stomach, she pulls down her skirt and adjusts her shorts around her waist. She's not careful enough. They flip pony-tailed heads towards their friends, the collective hiss of 'Did you see it?' slipping into sneezy giggles.

She turns away from their taunts towards her peg and begins a downward fumble with her shirt; fingers and buttons from the collar to her crotch. The bulge of her back pressed against the yellow fabric absorbs the spit of their titters, deepening the eagle-shaped sweat patch spreading its wings from shoulder to shoulder. Her bra is visible through the dampness, the tightness of its clasp clear to all who are looking. And everyone *is* looking. Always exposed; she has a lot more to show them.

Last button undone, she gently slips her arms out of the sleeves and leaves the blouse to rest on her shoulders. She keeps her movements steadied and her shoulders tensed. The shirt billows lightly around her in the stale air as she rummages inside her kit bag for her football shirt.

She's preoccupied with the precariousness of her cover and drops socks, tights, and tampons onto the floor. As she clumsily scoops them up again, her unhitched blouse flails behind her whilst she bends and rises, bends and rises, just as the wings of a swan extend and retract. Enthralled, yet no less appalled, by the performance, the girls clamp the edges of their noses between a finger and thumb, feigning offence at the air she's roused by it all. They've already switched their own shirts and slipped on their impractical skorts, making sure to flash ribcages and prominent spines in the process, to wiggle sharp hips and poke at flat bellies.

She finds her shirt at the gluey bottom of the bag and pulls it through the mouth the right way up for her immediate entry. She wrenches its scratchy material over her black bob, the faint grease in her hair lubricating her passage through the neck-hole. Ready, heart racing, she turns to face the room.

All eyes bore into her. They think the show is over, but it's only just begun. She clasps a dirty football boot beside either thigh, each loaded with studs and the potential for a streamlined shot to die for. The new season will begin in three weeks, and she is determined to make the team.

Coach clambers in, a slimy eye poking through shuttered fingers. He asks if they've all finished dressing. Most of them have, so that's enough. He barks positions and tactics over their make-up tips and snog stories. Indifferent to their tales, the feel of the ball already tingling in her feet, she's listening to Coach and nodding and stretching her hamstrings.

The training field is a mud bath. Her classmates are forced to sabotage their style for sweaty white bibs over their yellow shirts. They ooze as one into the less-puddled half of the pitch. From above, the scene looks gooey and chaotic, reminiscent of fried eggs dodging pouches of oil on a simmering pan. She, her once-bright socks now splattered in brown, approaches the other half, all set to stamp her footprints into its untouched surface.

Moments before, she had cushioned the goalkeeper's far-flung kick from the other end of the pitch into her jelly-thigh. Her skin had wobbled against the blow as she received it, yet quickly steadied the ball, easily embracive of the spherical body. The ball had sailed straight to her as if there were no other option and now it lies at the tip of her toes, obediently awaiting her touch.

Here she is, at the wonky spray of a halfway line, planning the attack.

Her mind is quick. She advances. The curve of her inner foot nurses the slippery ball, juggles it around the shy stabs of their delicate feet and taps it through the gaping widths between their spindly legs. She quickly peels away the first sheet of defence and approaches the layer behind, which, like a repellent magnet, moves two steps back for each one she takes forward. They veer to the left of the pitch as she bounds towards the right. The fog of their light shirt sleeves and skorts gathers like the frothy lip of a tide, drifting away from her front-crawl through the murky river, splashing backwards against the heavy slap of her feet through the dirt.

Her body is laughter. This is easy.

She's dancing on tiptoes along the sleek roll of the ball's hurtling glide, flirting in an accelerated waltz down the empty wing. The path towards the corner post has been laid especially for her. They're strides behind her pace and beginning to slow. She doesn't notice. Her eyes are preoccupied, flicking from her feet to the black and white blur of neatly stitched diamonds spinning between her boots.

They give up the chase, panting. All their efforts to catch up, compete, compare, are defeatedly resigned. She doesn't care. She's strides beyond, now, and sprinting towards the goal. Only rapidly closing space sits between her and the towering posts. She gobbles up the air and it funnels out behind her, expanding the vacancy between the flash of her silhouette and the bib-coloured residue of those left behind.

You need fuel, Coach had said. She didn't believe it. You need energy. She didn't want it. But then, she took a football to her feet. You need breakfast, lunch and dinner. Yes, she does. She needs to fill her plate and accept any seconds because between her lips and over her tongue pass delicious catalysts, tasty triggers to the violent swing of her arm out to the side as she prepares for the shot, the controlled withdrawal of her best leg from the ball's surface, the tensed ankle waiting to follow through her finest. She chomps and chews her means of victory and they are watching her, eyebrows raised, lips parted.

The goalkeeper's eyes are locked too firmly on the shooter to bother with the shot and the ball is devoured by the back of the net, slamming straight into the corner of its open mouth. The violent smash against the netting is palpable on her skin, like she and the ball had never let go. Crowds of goosebumps rise on her legs to greet the glory and something hits her too, internally; a rush of sweetness she cannot name.

She turns to face the way she has come. The ball, encaged in white fabric, hooks around the back pole and hangs in the air, swinging just a little, like a pendulum counting the seconds before the sound of the whistle. And even the high squeal of Coach's piercing blow doesn't cut through the weight of the scene collapsing over the field, halting each girl in her muddy tracks. The wind has calmed; the ball is stilling. The ghost of its sway will linger. Black and white bulge through the net, pitching diamonds in the grey sky.

JULIANN GUERRA

*Thrift Store Finds*

Watching Kenzie in a thrift store was like watching a lioness on the hunt, or so Madeline assumed. She seemed to tune out the outside world and zone in on the rack of sweaters, looking for her prey. In her own opinion, Madeline found the limited organization frustrating and the smell reminiscent of the nursing home her grandmother had lived in before she passed away. Thankfully, Madeline knew Kenzie would come looking for her once she made her selections, so she drifted over to the books and journals in the back corner of the store.

While this section of the thrift store had bookshelves, everything seemed to be thrown onto them haphazardly. Madeline picked up a few books, flipped them over to read their synopses, and then put them back on the shelf, making sure they were standing upright; an action she couldn't resist. Then she started looking at the different journals. Some were ones she had seen in other stores, some were lined, and some were leather-bound. The last one she picked up appeared to be handmade. It was sturdy, covered in a red fabric, and the pages were an off-white parchment, sewn in with purple thread.

Madeline was surprised to find that the journal wasn't empty inside, but rather, completely filled. As she flipped through the pages, Madeline saw worn cards, boarding passes, maps, pamphlets, and photographs. By the time Kenzie came to find her, Madeline was a quarter of the way through the journal, reading a card that was wishing the recipient a happy Thanksgiving and asking how she was going to celebrate since she wasn't in America.

"I found a sweater that's going to look so good on you while you tour college campuses," Kenzie said. "And look, the price tags are still on it!"

"Kenzie, look at this," Madeline said, showing her the journal. "It's someone's scrapbook. Why would someone donate this to a thrift store?"

"I don't know, but look at those dates. This thing is old. Maybe she died and all of her stuff got donated."

"What? Why would her family get rid of this?"

"Maybe she didn't have any family," Kenzie shrugged.

"I refuse to believe the owner of this journal didn't have at least one person in her life who wouldn't want to keep this."

"All right, fine," Kenzie said, taking the journal out of Madeline's hands and walking toward the front of the store.

"What are you doing?" Madeline asked, flinching slightly as she watched Kenzie drop the journal onto the counter with the rest of her finds.

"We both know you're not going to be able to let this go, so I'm going to buy it for you and then you're going to drive yourself crazy looking for someone to return it to."

The journal ended up costing two dollars. Madeline considered asking the man adding up their products if he knew who had donated it, but he didn't appear to be in the happiest of moods, spending a sunny Saturday afternoon working at a thrift store, so Madeline decided she'd count on the internet to give her the answers she wanted.

Once she was back home, Madeline read through the journal from cover to cover, picking out important details. She knew the person who made the scrapbook was Amelia Carson, who appeared to be not much older than Madeline in her photos, and clearly enjoyed being a tourist. She smiled with a baguette in front of the Eiffel Tower, made a funny face at a guard outside of Buckingham Palace, and took a pasta-making class in Italy. There were also group photos of her with friends and family. She collected coasters from her favorite pubs. She added captions, quotes, and comments reminding her of her favorite foods and locations in messy, print handwriting. She got a short haircut in February that had grown out by June.

After a few hours of searching, Madeline found three people she thought had the potential to be related to Amelia based on their location and social media: Carson Adams, Samantha Bradley, and Maggie Green. Madeline reached out to all of them to explain she found the journal and hoped one of them would be able to claim it. She attached a few photos of the journal and its contents so that one of them would be able to identify Amelia.

Days passed and Madeline hadn't heard anything back from the three people she had reached out to. She looked through the journal every night, telling herself that she was looking for more details that could help her find someone to give the journal back to, but she never went back online to share her findings.

Two weeks after Madeline's social media search, Samantha Bradley claimed the journal belonged to her grandmother and the two agreed to meet at a local coffee shop so Madeline could return it.

"I brought a few photos of my grandmother so you knew I was telling the truth," Samantha said with a small laugh as she pulled a folder out of her tote bag. She looked like Amelia had in the pictures taken in April of her trip, and around the same age. The biggest difference Madeline could see was that Samantha's hair was darker.

Madeline looked down at the images of Amelia—some were already in the journal, but others showed Amelia after her time in Europe. Some new ones included one of Amelia on her wedding day, one with her surrounded by what appeared to be her children and grandchildren, one at the Great Wall of China that couldn't have been too many years after Europe, and one of her and Samantha at Samantha's graduation.

"She seems like a lot of fun," Madeline said.

"Oh, she was something else, let me tell you. She loved to travel, but she was also a strong advocate for spending the rare day in your pajamas watching movies and eating as much junk food as possible."

"Well I'm sure she would want you to have this, more than she would want me to," Madeline said as she passed the scrapbook across the table. It felt strange passing the journal off to someone she had just met. Even though logically, Madeline understood that as Amelia's granddaughter, Samantha probably knew all of the stories within the journal and had seen the pictures, Madeline still couldn't help but feel like she was handing over a friend's secrets.

"The gap year book," Samantha said, flipping through the pages. "This had to be the adventure she talked about the most. It was her longest one.

She left right after she graduated and spent nearly a year and a half living away from home; learning, traveling, trying to gain as many experiences as she possibly could."

They continued to talk about Amelia's life, but also their own. Madeline explained how she was starting to tour college campuses and had to decide what type of schools she wanted to apply to. Samantha, who was finishing her senior year of college, gave her advice on what to look for and emphasized how fast time goes by. They chatted for about half an hour, but they always seemed to come back to Amelia.

"Every year for Christmas she would buy us an unlined journal, hoping the one from the year before was full of memories. And if any of us ever had to explain that we still had blank pages, she would say, 'They're not blank, they're simply waiting to collect your future memories.'" Samantha smiled down at her grandmother's scrapbook before looking up at Madeline. "I don't know how this journal ended up at that thrift store, but I am so happy you found it and made a point to return it to my family. And I'm glad you enjoyed looking through my grandmother's memories. There are going to be a ton of exciting things coming up in your life, Madeline, and the only advice I can give you is advice my grandmother would swear by: buy yourself a journal."

After they said goodbye and promised to stay in touch, Samantha left the coffee shop and Kenzie, who had been sitting a few tables back in fear of Madeline being misled by an internet predator, sat down in the now empty seat.

"That seemed to go well. I could only hear some of what you guys were talking about, but given how long you talked, it couldn't have been awful," Kenzie concluded.

"It did go well," Madeline agreed as she stood up and gathered her bag. "We need to stop at the store on the way home. I want to buy a journal."

## BETH GRAINGER

*Anchorless*

Quiet Sunday, the world still unconscious, I the same
wedged foetally between glove box and cup holder.
Shut eyes round the roundabout drifting
as someone else drives me forward *or back*.
Dying heather forms a blurred line un-buckled
out of my half open eye whilst an expert
on the radio proclaims the end of the earth.

Window open, hand dangling as a black sheep
raises his eyebrows invisibly.
Take me with them then, wash me away
in these last minutes before the dry-stone walls tumble
and the streams, turn to gutters.

BETH GRAINGER

*11.05AM: A Front Room in Hyde*

Rain peppers the grey flecks of her iris, her mind distracted
as her swollen mouth latches on to the teat of the wine bottle.

A foetus lies horizontally in her pouting stomach, inactive
while a dry tear skirts her cheek onto the carpet of the hostel.

She strokes the velvet baby-grow lovingly across her navel, deducted
from next Tuesday's advance entertaining *him*.

As the de-humidifier purrs on in slow torture
her fogged mind wonders absently whether it was a son, or daughter.

*10.06PM: Centre Line of the High Street, Hyde*

She balances delicate toes within the paint of the centre line, balletic
giggling childishly as a crowd of spectators begins to swell.

Car breaks screech and an Audi driver gets out, unapologetic.
Grazed kneed, she crawls on her elbows, sobbing, *Go to hell.*

A junior doctor rolls his eyes whilst injecting the anaesthetic
as she garbles proudly about a pair of tiny white mittens *real Chanel!*

They discharge her the next day, she's fine, from what they can assess
the NHS is, after all, under a significant amount of stress.

# BETH GRAINGER

## *Salford Ramble*

They're always in the water, the bodies. Absolutely no point looking or
sharing Facebook posts.
If they don't show up in two days that's it they're gone, drowned
unless of course,
it's an Honour Killing in which case you won't find them because they're
long gone now,
dead in Pakistan; more easily covered up than a semi's garden in
Oldham,
or in the port or the Quays that's where they might be if they're
white.
Jimmy drinks port, lashes it back in Smithy's with a suit on he thinks he's
distinguished.
Just pissed always has been, ever since she left him – anger that squirts
tomato ketchup
out of thin little packets the size of the fag that Lucy grits between
her teeth,
big buck teeth but not bigger than Jimmy's cock he thinks, he is a cock,
really.
She was too young for him, but he's young in the head, there's a
label
now, of-course there wasn't back then and he doesn't think he has it
*Foetal-Alcohol-Spectrum-Disorder*
or rather lots of disorders all boiling down to the fact you shouldn't
drink pregnant.
But Lucy does, only one glass a big one mind, of red every night but Sunday –
Monday morning –
she goes to see her mum at Bluebell's with chocolate ginger biscuits
and listens
quietly doesn't say a word just wants her to think that she's alright that

       the cycle's broken.

*Laurel*

"Work it out yourself," said Ms. Ross. That's what all of the teachers said those days at school. Any number of horrible things could be happening and if someone asked a teacher, she'd say "work it out yourself," assuming that whatever it was had to be trivial. However, that was never the case. I would normally walk around on my own, or pick up bugs to put in my pail. But today I decided I would sit in a sandbox under a tree and dig by where the teachers usually gossiped. However, this futile activity of scooping sand into a pail became trite. So I assumed my regimen of going on a walk. I passed by the other children playing tag or pretending to be horses, their faces plastered with an expression of utmost elation. It was the unadulterated joy of childhood that I knew the teachers always talked about. I didn't remember anything other than childhood. I didn't remember being a baby. I didn't remember.

I found myself as usual alone, wishing I had a book. I had to wait for teachers to leave books by the benches—that was the only way I could read. I saw them berate the other children for reading and force them to play. This usually resulted in skinned knees and uniforms stained green by the grass. Chlorophyll, I once heard. But once, I was blessed with serendipity and a teacher left *Emma* by Jane Austen on the bench. I took it and read it behind the library building. Nobody seemed to notice my absence.

Once during recess, I was making my way back to the sandbox when two boys approached me. Their uniforms askew and stained with not only mud and dirt, but tomato sauce and violent grass. Their shoes untied and arms adorned with scabs. White shirts with missing buttons, the woven pieces of their belts deteriorating before my very eyes like decomposing flesh. I wondered why they had approached me.

"I bet we could fit you in a cabinet!" They laughed, and I watched their arms reach for me.

After that, I decided to only speak to people I knew I could trust. I made myself unseen. It was an easy solution. I don't know why nobody else ever thought to do it.

I was often drawn to a tiny girl who was also alone, but never berated for reading. She had black hair that made her look like a mushroom, and legs so skinny they looked like they could snap. She wore a blue headband and looked for acorns to feed to the squirrels. I often saw the other children pick on her. I did not say a word. I was unseen. She caught ladybugs every day.

Then I saw the girl with a face peppered with mud-like freckles step on her ladybugs. I went back to look at them. Waxy and crimson, they scrambled across the pavement. I kept them in my pocket and named them Pebble and Sally.

I walked out one day onto the withered fallen leaves to see the new building had been completed. I watched them build it for a year. Beams of steel, violent looking machines. Men with yellow hard hats. It made me very sad—like there was a malignant gape in me. I don't know why. I used to sit and weep watching them build over the bayou, as if a piece of me was being murdered. I tried to remember the white majestic egrets, and the raccoons that smelled like wet rocks. I felt the mud between my toes and the smell of cypress trees reminded me of my mother. She used to sing to me when I was only three instead of seven. She put cherry laurel leaves in my curly blond hair and taught me that if you tear it up and rub it together your hands will smell like cherries. She taught me and my friend Molly. I would weep even more if I thought about them. Now, the building was finally complete. There are so many levels and lifeless, oppressive gray. The other children run in and out happily. Why can't they remember what it was like before? And then sometimes I thought—why can't I?

Everyone was prohibited from going beyond the black wire fence. But nobody ever noticed when I went. I tried to look for egrets, but most of them were gone. Once beyond the fence, I saw a little boy struck by poison ivy. His skin bubbled, looking porous and red as if it was boiling. A teacher found him and admonished him for going behind the fence. How could such a tiny hole fit his plump body, she wondered. But the boy was crying and scratching his skin until it turned a red that seemed familiar to me. Nevertheless, I always found myself wandering around the bayou. *Or what was left of it.* I went to find poison ivy but there was no bubbling.

The teachers would often speak into small black squares with buttons on them—I called them echo squares. Sometimes for the entire duration of recess, walking the same stretch of grass under the oak tree until the grass was completely flattened. "That's how they are at this age," they would scoff, their painted fingernails tapping the echo square. I would speak into the trees I encountered, but would never hear a response. I made my own echo square out of tree bark and clay. I liked to pretend that someone answered me—maybe my mother. But nothing came. I tapped my echo square and watched as some of the clay particles flaked off and fell to the ground. The smell of wet mud made me sad.

One day, I saw the tiny girl standing by the fence alone. I noticed that she was pulling leaves through the holes. She pulled out the waxy leaves and crushed them in her hands and smelled them. Cherry laurel. I was not the only one who knew of its olfactory benefits. I decided that she was worthy. I saw her shove some of the leaves into her pockets. I wondered where she took them.

I often found myself wandering around the bathroom on the fourth floor trying to remember what it used to feel like when it was the bayou. Now it was a bathroom with a high ceiling encased in white glossy squares. Glittering stone and spouts of water. Navy opaque doors. Thick but lightweight. Suddenly, the door opened, and the tiny girl came in. Today, her headband was silver. I would not be unseen today. I mustered up my courage and sang.

"*La la la la-la.*"

She looked around the bathroom frantically.

"Hello?" she asked, confused.

"What's your name?" I smiled.

"*Hello?*" she asked again, walking around, pushing open all the navy doors as if she were looking for something. Maybe I had remained unseen for too long.

"*La la la la-la,*" I sang. She heard my song once more, but walked right past me. I need to practice being seen again.

I saw the leaves change from green to brown. I saw the white bark fall off of the crepe myrtle trees. I saw the children come in and out with scarves and hats on. I know she heard me. But she never spoke to me. I wanted so badly for her to be my friend because nobody else noticed me. I wandered around and sang for a while, waiting for the tiny girl to finally notice me until one day she spoke.

"My mother said that I'm supposed to tell you to go into the light," she said, staring at the mirror and speaking into the open space of the bathroom. Perhaps I had made a mistake. I felt a tear fall down my cheek.

"You're confused," I explained. "But I'll make sure nothing bad happens to you." I didn't sing to her again after that.

When all the children were gone and new children appeared as they often did, I sat in the sandbox digging as I always did with Pebbles and Sally playing on my arm. It was winter once more and the children shivered in their turtlenecks, running around like ants. They laughed and played ball. Their noses pink and lips purple. There were more grass stains and more scabs. The teachers had not left a book out in a very long time. I felt myself beginning to think the same way the children spoke—without all the new words I had learned from *Emma*.

"Be careful!" said Ms. Ross, coming up to the edge of the sandbox to warn a girl named Helen. "The wind is always so strong here! Sand might get in your eyes. Look at those shovels and pails being moved by the wind! It looks like they're moving themselves!" She pointed to where I was digging.

# NIKOLA DIMITROV

*Eksploding Sun*

I do not know what was said, what horrific, biased half-truths were shouted in the darkness from both sides of the flickering candles on the dinner table. All I know is the anger I saw in Tom's eyes later that rainy evening as he knocked on my door, soaking.

"What happened to you?!"

"Can I stay over tonight?" His tone was casual. A half-smile illuminated his face. "Are you wearing pajamas?"

"They're comfy," I said as I stepped away and let him enter my small apartment. "Why are you here?"

"I had an argument with Dad."

"What about?"

"You know, stuff."

I raised an eyebrow.

"He keeps trying to shove his beliefs in my face. I couldn't take it anymore."

I went to the bathroom and fetched a towel for him to dry off. "Ah, the age-old question about the existence of God. Why do you even try to have that conversation with him? I thought we agreed to let it go."

"Well... I have proof now."

"Yeah, right. And I have a pet T-Rex."

"Shut up, *Professor*," he said mockingly and threw my towel at me. "If you go and pick up my stuff from Dad's place tomorrow, I'll show you."

"I'm giving a lecture on quantum mechanics."

"Boring."

"You're not going back?" I asked.

"Nah, man. I'm sick of that place."

"What are you going to do for money?"

"Dunno. We'll see. I was planning on staying with you until I figure it out," he said, then added smugly, "if that's okay."

For a future Nobel Prize winner, my little brother wasn't what one would call smart. Not in the conventional sense. In all the years I've known him, Tom never exhibited levels of attention span or emotional intelligence beyond those of a twelve-year-old. What distinguished him from the average seventh grader was his highly developed sense of insignificance. He knew with vigorous certainty and from a very early age that life was meaningless and there wasn't any higher purpose, grand design, or ultimate goal to our existence.

I remember the long nights we spent talking as kids. I would lie on the top bunk bed, looking up at the plastic stars we had glued to the ceiling, listening to his disembodied voice washing over me from all sides.

"Sam, we live on a ball of rocks and mud," he said one night. "We are rotating around the sun. It is like a giant fire is what Mr. Thompson told me. One day it will explode, and everyone will die." All of this he delivered in an even, matter-of-fact tone.

"Even Dad?"

"Even us."

Mr. Thompson was our primary school science teacher. I suspect he was the one who planted the idea in Tom's head that with a few modifications to his bike and given sufficient velocity, he could fly off the roof of the garage. The following morning, Tom procured wooden planks under the pretext that we were building a treehouse. Instead, what we built was an elaborate runway for him and his flying machine. After many sketches of the mechanics behind the stunt, drawings of the trajectories of his flight, and projections of where he and the bike would land, we were ready.

The wings were in place, the runway at a perfect fifteen-degree slope, and I was sitting on the bike, tightening the screws one last time. Tom took a marker and wrote "Eksploding Sun" on my helmet.

"What are you doing?" I asked suspiciously.

He smiled deviously, put the helmet on my head, and gave me a push.

•

In retrospect, I think Tom was right. I suppose I should have looked up, seen the murdering ball of hydrogen in the sky, sat on the ground, and just waited for my time to come. This was, he said to me once, the most sensible way to go about this futile existence that was forced upon us. Nevertheless, grudgingly, Tom kept at it. Living. Waking up, putting on a pair of pants and a shirt, and scribbling away.

Now that we were sharing the same flat again, I was reminded of his multiple quirks. The dirty clothes, the empty cereal boxes, his general disregard for people. For Tom, everything revolved around his work.

What he called his "work" consisted of him pouring the stream of consciousness which he was no longer able to contain onto the pages of his diaries. He wrote frantically, illegibly, disregarding punctuation, spelling, page orientation. He began sentences in one language, then switched to another halfway. He drew charts, jotted equations, analyzed trajectories. My floor was covered in his dirty socks and the walls and ceiling in scribbles.

"Most people never come to terms with the fact they are at the mercy of nature," Tom said to me over the muffled sound of loud music coming from the next room. We were celebrating his 30th birthday. "Think about it," he continued, gesturing wildly and spilling beer over my shirt. "For millennia we've known the ultimate fate that awaits us. Death is inevitable. Yet, for some reason, we keep crawling inside our concrete labyrinths, illuminated by our artificial suns, and busy ourselves with our insignificance."

"All of us except for you, brother," I said.

"We meet people, talk of art, passion, love, money, sex, politics, and all these other abstract ideas that prevent us from coming to terms with our transience. Worst of all are people like Dad. He has no concept of empirical evidence. Neither do the rest of his sect, for that matter. In an attempt to suppress their existential dread, they convinced themselves of the existence of a bearded man in the sky who watches them when they masturbate."

I choked on my beer. "I thought he overreacted by kicking you out. I get it now."

"Not only that, but in addition to him being the all-knowing and all-powerful creator of the universe, the bearded man in the sky is also apparently very poor, so people need to donate so he can build golden church domes and giant crosses. Otherwise, they burn in hell for the rest of eternity."

"I thought you debunked God already."

"Yeah, I've been meaning to talk to you about that." Tom paused and looked down at his feet. "I was thinking maybe I could use the lab?"

"The university laboratory? Not happening, bro."

"I'll let you publish my work under your name," he insisted. "You are *the professor*, after all. Come on, bro. I just need the spectrograph."

"You are planning to solve one of the biggest philosophical quandaries humanity has faced using a spectrograph?" I asked, pausing. "Meet me at the entrance tomorrow at five."

Eventually I did present Tom's work under my name. My only contribution, despite the fact that the Nobel Prize was technically assigned to me, was fixing Tom's spelling.

We had an argument over the title, but in the end he had his way. *Where Is Your God Now?* was published in the winter of 2030 and was essentially an expansion of quantum theory. It was a beautiful piece of scientific enquiry, a triumph of rationality over wishful thinking. Tom had deduced, purely by extrapolating from the known laws of the quantum world, that the fundamental building blocks of matter had one more characteristic in addition to spin and position. They had a life cycle. If his theory was correct, the elements of the periodic table would slowly start to disintegrate in order from lightest to heaviest. Hydrogen and helium would be the first to go, so he directed the university equipment at the sun and recorded a shift in its luminosity, consistent with his hypothesis.

That meant the inevitable heat death of the universe will result not from proton decay billions of years in the future, but from a decay of the Higgs field. In only a couple of decades, the stars in the night sky will extinguish, one by one. Our sun's fuel supply will run out and our home star will become a mere ball of iron and nickel. No longer trapped in its gravity well, the planets of the solar system will shoot off in different directions, embarking on solitary journeys in a dark and lifeless universe. Humanity will bear witness to none of it, as the very atoms that make up our bodies will disintegrate into nothingness along with our dying sun.

We have thirty years before the God particle leaves our plane of existence forever.

As far as I am aware, Dad and Tom haven't said a word to each other ever since my brother stormed out. All I know is that one day I came home to find a piece of paper in my dad's handwriting sitting on my dining table. The note read:

*For dust thou art, and unto dust shalt thou return.*
*Genesis 3:19*

# SHYLA TAPSCOTT

*A Princess's Lament*

How much longer, hero? Before you set me free?

I wonder if you can feel my presence within these walls. You stride into the ruins of the castle, of my quarters, where no one has trespassed in over a century. The corrupt, one-eyed machine blocking the stairs, warding away any traveler or looter less brave than you, hero, lies crumpled and disassembled now. Its gears and screws strewn across the steps, marking your trail into my quarters.

You defeat the eight-foot-tall, pig-snouted creature that lingers near the hearth with two definite hits, not a bead of sweat or trace of strain upon your flushed face. Without the monster's grunts echoing across the stone walls, it's eerily silent. Even the ancient machines, akin to the many I've witnessed you defeat, hover outside quietly, their whirrs stalled in time.

You sheathe that legendary sword with all the care of a father with an infant child, and perhaps it deserves it. A breath—your breath, hero—and you turn toward the wreckage of what was once my bed, now overturned and broken in on itself. Above where the headboard used to rest is a gilded portrait frame caging my splintered visage. It hangs awry, covered in large cobwebs like decorative silk doilies. You hoist yourself over the ruins and stray toward the portrait. Leather-gloved fingers caress the canvas and smooth it down, suturing the seam that tears my face in two, and then I am whole. At least in your eyes.

There, however, within irises blue as the tunic upon your body, I cannot find recognition. My face means nothing to you. I am a piece of art. But then your eyebrows furrow and you tilt your head to the left, as you used to. Maybe I have not been entirely forgotten!

I say your name in excitement and my power palpitates. The voice you've come to know as mine, usually within your head, leaks through the cracks in the stone walls, floating on the beams of late afternoon sunlight that illuminate the dust. You follow its sound to the corner of the room, where a moth-eaten desk still stands, shrouded in drawings of the autonomous machines prowling the castle grounds even now. A diary's pages, open, rustle in the breeze until one is turned. My power now spent, I resume my omnipotent seat and watch from the celestial void I reside in as you approach the diary. I do not have to hear you read it aloud to know what it says, for my loops and scrawls are still legible, though perhaps not familiar to you.

Do you truly not remember, hero, how I hated your presence at first? You followed my every move like a puppy, though admittedly a less excited one. Always at a distance, always silent. I loathed the idea of needing a protector. But when you singlehandedly fought off a band of rebels assailing me, with no thought for your own life, I realized how much I truly did need you watching my back. Instead of hating you for it, as would have been expected of my unamended character, I unfolded before you. For I could not blame you for following your destined path when mine refused to reveal itself to me.

Your eyebrows furrow once more, a betrayal to your usually formidable stoicism, and I know without looking which diary entry you've run across. Memories we share, memories you have yet to retrieve, filter into my disembodied mind. They contain heartbreak, disappointment, and ultimately, failure: all entirely on my part. If I'd only learned then how to harness the power the goddess bestowed upon me, to restrain the inevitable darkness sooner, the land would never have gone to waste. The castle would not be beguiled in impenetrable, growing tragedy. The kingdom would not be pregnant with terrors of the night and signs of a repeat of the calamity that destroyed it a century before. And you, hero, would still remember me.

You close your eyes and lift the diary shut. I follow you as you scale the inside wall, where the spiral staircase used to stand, and clamber into the turret. Slinking against the wall, watching for the hovering machine above to continue its predictable path, you wait for it to disappear behind the tower opposite you and then sprint across the bridge connecting the two. The machine's pink searchlight crests the wall of the bridge just as the echo of your hammering footsteps slap against the stone bridge. It senses you, but you're safely within the tower walls when its laser fires, blowing loose bricks from the exterior.

It is a small space, but it served well for my research. Though the desk in my quarters is a mess of half-finished sketches and pages of scribbled thoughts, the study you stand in now is a terror. Yellowed, ragged pages litter the ground and shelves, some still nailed to the eroded stone walls. Books and scrolls lie on the ground where they toppled off shelves. Poetry. Literature. Mechanics. Local history. In truth, nothing has changed in a century. You kneel in one particular pile of rubble where decades of decay somehow nurtured growth, and with your fingertips, touch the petals of the single flower growing there. It is a rare, beautiful type of flora: blue and white and hard to grow in captivity. The Silent Princess.

Hero, recall what I told you about that particular flower. How rare it was to successfully cultivate, and now it blossoms even in the midst of ruin. Your hand wavers near the bend in the thin stem, but as if on second thought, you leave it embedded in the soil and ruin to continue to thrive. Perhaps your memories are not lost. Just dormant. If I'd a physical body, my heart would warm within my chest.

You thumb through my research journal, decidedly faster than you did my diary, and then sigh. The light grows richer, darker, through the tower's broken shutters. It reflects off the rusted telescope, throwing an ancient light upon the flower. You climb the debris and shelving to peer out of the broken shutters. The snow-peaked mountains rise in the distance beyond the castle ruin, yellowed by the setting sun. Soon it will be dark, and the night terrors will ascend, springing from beneath the soil where they rest dormant during the day. You will have to find lodging to avoid them, though I know their existence does little to worry you.

Soon is too soon. You descend the exterior of the tower, brick by exposed brick, avoiding the neon searchlight of the hovering machine in the dark, and drop into the moat below. With every foot you put between us, every stroke you cut through the water, I feel the distance keenly. You know, hero, I was but a few halls away, growing weaker in my attempt to contain the darkness within the castle walls. A famished terror, maw salivating at the prospect of devouring the kingdom lest I fail. But you are not prepared yet. And you must not fail, either.

How much longer must I wait before you set me free? Another day, another week, another year? Wait, trapped in the sanctum of the castle that has not provided me peace for over a century, keeping the evil at bay until you are ready. Light fighting darkness. Ready to take back what is ours, wielding that legendary sword. Ready to avenge the fallen champions and prevent the loss of the innocent thriving now, even in the desolation. Ready to answer the call of the uninhibited wild which acts as teacher where I cannot.

As you climb the steep shore onto a hill overlooking the prison ruins to the west, you turn to look at the castle shrouded in darkness. Not just a darkness born of night, but a darkness born of an evil our land has known over and over for ten thousand years.

I have faith you will free us from this ancient scourge, as your ancestors have before you—as the prophecy tells. A one-hundred-year slumber has done nothing to weaken your innate skill and courage. Nothing but erase your memories. Yet, even without them, you know what must be done. It is up to you to fulfill your duty though I failed to fulfill mine. Then, and only then, will this all be over.

*Then.* That moment in time when princess and her knight shall be reunited. When the kingdom is saved and once again at peace. When old, weary spirits of the fallen are put to rest.

Until then, hero, I shall continue to wait.

*Chicken Soup*

A cold winter day. The sun was flickering in the clouds. Poultry walked out of his office, and he was exhausted.

In modern society, the world is colourless, and people are mindless livestock who are held captive by the illusion of money's supremacy. Everyone lives a hard life, the sole purpose of which is to accumulate wealth and have no fun. Thoughts were flying. Poultry was upset and wanted to breathe some fresh air. He saw a billboard at the bus stop: An artificial lake? It was a great place to go! He decided to have a look.

He walked into the underpass and found it was too dark. Maybe the lights were broken. He opened his mobile phone's flashlight and illuminated the way forward. The underpass was very long. He was walking, walking, like walking into a monster's oesophagus. He laughed at himself. He was a man who had no vitality. Even dogs wouldn't bite him!

Finally, when Poultry reached the exit, he turned off the flashlight and tripped over a mineral water bottle. He fell and banged his head on the ground.

'Fuck!' Poultry got up and began to stomp on the bottle. When he had calmed down, he walked gloomily to the park.

There was nothing special in the park. Just a row of trees and an icy lake. Poultry did not see the beautiful scenery he wanted to see, and a smouldering gas stuck in his chest.

'Cluck.' A strange noise came from somewhere. Poultry listened quietly, then searched around. Wow! A fat Luhua chicken!

He recalled the chicken soup that his mother cooked for him when he was a child living in a small village. When Mom scooped the chicken soup from the casserole pan into the bowl, the smell was instantly arousing to his appetite. The way the yellow chicken oil would dot the clear soup, and the way the skin on the chicken feet was cooked slightly, and the yam boiled soft, as fresh as the first snow...

That smell, that taste, that desire.

Since he had come to the big city to study in college, he had never been able to taste that kind of pure happiness. At that time, he ate takeout every day. After graduation, he worked as hard as he could and there was no time to relax to enjoy food.

In his limited life, he had been asked by his parents to come to the big city to have a better future; he had been urged by his teacher to find a good job to survive; he had been compared with his colleagues and told he had to work hard, or he would be fired. He never had a dream of his own.

No.

He wanted to catch the chicken. He wanted to take it home and make a bowl of chicken soup.

This chicken ignited the fire in his life. For the first time, he had a dream and the strength to pursue it.

The wind blew, blowing away the leaves, blowing over the clouds, and blowing out the sun.

The only thing in Poultry's eyes was the chicken.

He chased after the chicken, and even smashed the frozen lake with his mobile phone when he tried to throw it at the chicken. His blood was boiling. He felt like he was burning! Is this how it feels when someone has a dream? He was a stranger to this feeling.

He made a simple trap with branches to catch the chicken. At first, the chicken was overwhelmed by the branches, but when he was going to seize the chicken, it flapped its wings and broke through the branches. Poultry's hands pressed to the ground through those branches. His hands were immediately bloodstained.

Instead of being angry, he smiled. This pain made him inexplicably happy.

Would he be happy if he could do what he wanted to do, even if he failed? Or was it because his dream-pursuing heart was so firm, that even if he failed, it would not affect his good mood? He felt the vitality in his body, his heart, his soul. He was no longer mindless livestock. Poultry devoted himself to catching the chicken.

He suddenly came up with an idea. He could lure the chicken to the icy lake and, when it slipped, he would use his scarf to trip it over, and catch it. That was a wonderful idea! The fire in his soul burned more vigorously.

Poultry went back to the underpass and got the mineral water bottle. He spent two hours in the park looking for bugs, filling the bottle, and sprinkling them on the road to the icy lake. Eventually, he went after the chicken and drove it towards the bugs. The chicken was so stupid. It pecked the bugs and walked to the icy lake.

Now!

Poultry rushed onto the ice, and threw his scarf around the chicken. The chicken slipped and hit its head on the ice.

Ha-ha, delicious chicken soup! He was overjoyed.

Unexpectedly, the ice cracked, and he slammed into the cold water.

Upon the ice, the innocent chicken went away.

Under the ice, Poultry struggled fiercely, struggled constantly, struggled desperately.

He tried his best to reach up to the shining golden world.

All in vain.

*The Girl from the Sky*

"This weekend was like any ordinary weekend," Natalie began, bouncing on her toes in excitement. "I helped Grandma with some gardening and started reading a new book, but then..." She paused, surveying the bland expressions on her classmates' faces. "Yesterday a girl fell out of the sky and landed on my trampoline. She told us all about her world in the clouds and I took her to the park where I showed her all my favorite flowers and she told me the name of every bird we saw. Then, we had my grandma's chili and I gave her some chocolate, which she had never had before. And now, me and Grandma have to help her return home!" Natalie beamed at her crowd.

"That was very creative, Natalie. But the assignment was to tell us what you did this weekend, not to create a fictional story," Mrs. Marshall said.

"But I didn't!" Natalie protested.

Several students laughed and rolled their eyes. Natalie plopped into her seat and sulked while the rest of the students finished their weekend reports. Natalie found them all to be incredibly boring. Each filled with stories about running errands with parents, riding bikes, or playing games at home. Natalie was in the midst of a real-life adventure, and no one cared, or even believed her.

The moment the bell rang, Natalie burst out of her seat and dashed toward the door, staying ahead of the throng of students filling the hallway. She pushed the door open and scanned the parking lot furiously. Her grandmother pulled her truck up to the curb, ignoring the honks from other cars full of parents maneuvering the crowded parking lot. Natalie ran to the car and jumped into the back seat.

"Where is she?" Natalie asked.

Her grandmother lurched the car forward. "I left her at home. I thought that this many people might be a bit much for her."

The truck pulled into the driveway ten minutes later. The house was small and obscured from the road by an overgrown flower garden bursting in full bloom. When Natalie and her grandmother entered the house, they found the girl from the sky sitting on the couch anxiously awaiting their arrival. Natalie couldn't help but marvel at the figure before them. The girl's skin and thick curls were a shade of brilliant blue that matched the sky outside. She was wearing an oversized t-shirt and jean shorts that Natalie's grandmother had lent her—her own clothes had begun to evaporate shortly after her landing on the trampoline.

"Natalie! You are home!" The girl's voice was a soft whistle through the air.

She jumped up and wrapped her vibrant arms around Natalie.

"So, what's the plan?" Natalie asked, looking up at her grandmother. "How are we going to help her get home?"

"With the help of the wind, of course!" The girl smiled down at her.

"There is a storm coming in this afternoon and we spent the day checking wind patterns," Natalie's grandmother explained. "If we can get her into a good wind gust, it should send her home."

"Then what are we waiting for!" Natalie squealed.

"No one can rush the wind, Natalie," the girl from the sky said. "And first, we should harvest some mint from the garden. It is impolite to ask the winds for such a favor without bringing them a gift."

The three of them tramped out into the backyard with a jar that Natalie's grandmother had found under the kitchen sink. They settled themselves on the ground next to a bush of mint and began filling the jar with its leaves.

"Will you tell me the story of the city in the clouds?" Natalie asked. "And your great fall?"

"You already made her tell you the story three times yesterday," her grandmother chided.

"It's all right," the girl from the sky said, smiling sweetly. "Way up above your heads is another world. It is a world that exists not within but shimmering on top of this one. In the depths of what you see as clouds are large cities built from mist—with gardens, pathways, and towering buildings. Within these dwellings live my people, the people of the sky. We step lightly and are granted access to this in-between world. The winds push us across the skies, showing us the wide world, and within the rains we are continuously rejuvenated and gifted extended life. I live in a community that tends to storms and grows new clouds to add to our city."

The girl from the sky's eyes glazed over and she let one hand sink into the grass, curling the blades around her fingers. "While working in a distant garden patch, I allowed myself to become distracted by a window to your world which the winds pushed open before me. I was mesmerized by the vivid green and speeding people and cars. I have rarely had the opportunity to see the world below my feet and I could not look away. I must have stepped too close, for the next thing I knew, I was tumbling from my home. Despite its best efforts, the wind could only slow my descent. I thought I was surely lost when I landed on your trampoline." The girl from the sky smiled at Natalie. "And that is how I came to meet such lovely new friends."

As the girl finished her story, Natalie saw that her skin had changed from vibrant blue to an ever-darkening gray. She looked up and saw that the foretold storm was quickly moving toward them across the sky.

"It is time to go," her grandmother said, standing.

The little group grabbed the mint leaves and their coats and were soon piled into the truck, moving speedily down the road. They headed to a hill that stood just outside of town and was the highest point that they could think of to send the girl from the sky up with the wind.

By the time the car pulled into the gravel parking lot at the trailhead, the wind was swirling around them, throwing leaves and pine needles around their feet. The dark gray clouds blocked all the light from the sun. The girl's skin and hair matched their ominous surroundings and Natalie thought she looked like a goddess of storms.

They raced up the trail and as Natalie looked up at the girl beside her, her resolve broke.

"I don't want you to go," Natalie whimpered, her voice barely audible.

The girl from the sky took Natalie's hand tightly in her own as they walked. Natalie could see tears streaking down her face.

"I cannot stay," the girl said.

"But..." Natalie began.

"Look," her grandmother interrupted her, pointing to the girl from the sky.

It took Natalie a moment to understand but she finally realized that the girl was fading at her edges. Natalie rubbed her eyes but still the girl from the sky seemed to be evaporating into the air.

"I cannot last here."

"Maybe you could come visit for Christmas. You really have to try some hot chocolate," Natalie pleaded.

After a moment's hesitation, the girl from the sky said, "I will try."

"You won't forget me?" Natalie begged.

"Never. Thank you for my adventure."

When they reached the summit of the hill, a large swath of grass spilled out before them, the blades dancing wildly in the wind. Natalie could feel the wind pulling the girl from the sky away from her and clasped her hand tighter.

Next to them, Natalie's grandmother opened the jar of mint and began scattering it in the breeze. It swirled around them and filled their noses with its sweet scent.

"It's time!" she called to them.

The girl from the sky stepped forward and turned her head up toward the clouds. She smiled at Natalie and then at her grandmother. Natalie's eyes widened as she watched the girl being pulled from the ground, floating before them. The wind whipped playfully at her hair and then she was swept upwards. A tear rolled from Natalie's cheek, but the wind gently wiped it away. Her grandmother pulled her into her arms and the two watched until the girl from the sky disappeared above them.


Days passed and routine returned all too easily. No one at school asked Natalie about the girl from the sky and Natalie didn't try and bring it up with anyone but her grandmother.

One night, Natalie was awoken from sleep by the howling of the wind outside her bedroom window. She crawled over and leaned her forehead against the glass. The trees outside creaked as they swayed from side to side. Large raindrops ran down the glass. Natalie peered at the drops curiously as they began to move into a pattern across the window. Natalie smiled; the raindrops spelled out *Hello! I miss you!* Natalie breathed out, fogging up the glass, and wrote *I miss you too*.

# BRUNA CASTELO BRANCO

*Bye, Tereza*

Whenever I picture a funeral, I picture a rainy or cloudy day. Grey feelings match grey landscapes. But today is a beautiful, sunny day. It's a day of happiness and joy and sand and sandcastles and beaches and waves and surfers. But my sister, Tereza, is in a coffin about to be buried forever. And I think that the summer heat should show some respect for us. It should be raining. It's raining inside.

When you have a twin, you have a mirror. Better said, you're a mirror. We are so alike that even some relatives can't tell who is who sometimes. Our black, straight hair and fringe are the same. So is our thin voice – some people say it's annoying – and the way we walk too. Even our food preferences are similar: we love pizza, bread, broccoli and roasted potatoes, and we hate beans, pasta, apples and baked potatoes. At school, we are good at biology and terrible at maths. I mean, we were. I liked being a mirror. But now I'm just me.

Adam is here with his family. Tereza had been in love with him since we were six. When we were old enough – fourteen, probably – she would have been his girlfriend. I can't even look at Adam. I'm angry with him right now. He's a reminder that I'll turn fourteen alone. And thirteen. And twelve. And, in twenty-eight days, eleven. Our plan was to celebrate on a boat. But we can't do that anymore because she'll be under the ground.

When she got sick and stopped attending classes, Adam was worried. He is great at maths – the best in class – but he stopped raising his hand every time Miss Judite asked a question. When I told Tereza this, she looked happy for the first time in a while. She even smiled. She was already at the hospital and smiles were not common there. 'See! I told you he loved me. I miss him so much, Cecília. Do you think his mother would bring him here for a visit?' she asked, and I thought it unlikely because of all the germs he could get, but I didn't tell her that.

By that time, we were not mirrors anymore. My cheeks were redder than hers, and she had deep dark circles under her brown eyes. She was skinnier and looked like she was always tired. I could see every single bone in her fingers. It was ugly and scary, but I still wanted to look like her. So I stopped eating. Dad soon realised what I was doing and interrupted my plans. 'I don't need two sick daughters now,' he said. He had dark circles under his eyes too.

Adam was the only one in class who could distinguish between Tereza and me, and I never knew how. Tereza said that it was because they were in love and they would get married as soon as they turned eighteen. That was the only difference between us: she had her entire life planned and perfectly scheduled, while I didn't even know what I wanted to do for the next holidays. I'm the indecisive mirror. And now, I'll have to figure everything out alone.

When we were little, we liked to wear the same clothes or at least the same colours. Our favourite colour back then was yellow. This changed the day we learned about the complementary colours at school two years ago. Mr Setaro said that complementary colours fulfilled one another, so when Tereza wore orange, I wore blue, and when she wore red, I wore green, and when she wore yellow, I wore violet. It was hard to do this sometimes because we would have to have lots of colourful clothes, but it was fun to try. Mom and Dad wanted to help us, and we got some new clothes that Christmas. It was the best part of being two. An *only* person could never do something like that.

Other kids from school used to laugh at us. The boy I was in love with, Lucas, said we looked stupid.

'I thought that wearing the same colours every day was stupid enough, but look at you now!' he said. Everybody laughed, and I was about to cry in front of them when Tereza took my hand and guided me to the girls' toilet.

'If you want to cry, let's do it here. They don't deserve to feel so powerful.' I cancelled my love for him at that instant and I admired her for being so much smarter and more mature than those boys. I loved it when she was the bigger sister, even if I was born three minutes before her. And I loved her for making better choices and loving the nicest boy in school.

I think we're doing the complementary-colours thing now. I'm wearing black at her funeral, and she's wearing white in her coffin. I don't remember if black and white are complementary colours, but they're obviously opposite and it looks like one complements the other. But, today, I wish we were using the same colours, just like old times. I read once in a graphic novel called *Toutinegra* that accepting someone is gone is accepting that 'never again'. It's true. I'd like us to be two for life, but that's not happening. Never again. I'll soon be eleven, and she'll be ten forever. My hair will grow, my body will change, and she'll remain a child. I hate my body now, and I promise I'll hate it as long as I live and just because I live. I'm an ex-twin, so I'm nobody. And I regret not wearing white and the same crown of white roses Tereza is wearing today. If Tereza were here, she would have reminded me to arrange that.

The funeral is over, and now it's time to close the coffin and cover it with earth. So, it's the last time I'll see her ever and I wish it was raining. I see her pale face and closed eyes and white roses crown and I'm afraid of forgetting her. For some months, I'll see her in the mirror whenever I see me, but I know that's going to change soon. So I'm looking at her and trying not to blink but my eyes are hurting and I have to blink and it's so hot today. We're all sweating in these dark heavy clothes, and deep down I feel that I want it to be over soon so I can go to a cool place. I'm not crying, and nobody seems to understand why. Mom says I'm in shock. But what they don't know is that I'd been crying every night and morning since Tereza was sent to the hospital. Now, I'm drained. And I hate myself for that.

They are burying the coffin, and I remember the day we learned about moles in biology class. Moles are one of the loneliest species on the planet. They spend most of their life underground. They dig their own holes, and they make sure it's small enough so that no other mole can fit in there and they can be alone. They're lonely because they want to be, and I never understood how they could survive like that.

Devils Hole pupfish are alone too. But unlike moles, they have no option. They live isolated from the world in Devils Hole, a deep dark cave in a desert somewhere in the United States. We read a BBC Earth article once that said that there are just fifty of them and they all live together in a place the same size as a living room. Tereza loved reading about them. We planned to visit Devils Hole before she married Adam to see their living room – or at least try because we probably wouldn't be able to see anything.

Everybody says pupfish are the loneliest creatures in the world, but I still think that moles are lonelier. Pupfish are isolated from other species, but they're alone together, and they are all twins and triplets and brothers and sisters, all tiny blue things with the same face and family. They're mirrors. Tereza and I used to be like them at school: lonely and isolated, but together. The moles are all alone, though. They have brothers and sisters and mothers and fathers but remain alone. Are they happy? I hope I can find some moles one day and talk to them and ask them if they're happy. And how.

Now I look at Tereza's almost-buried coffin, and I see how her hole is big enough just for her, and I think she's a mole, but one that didn't choose to be alone. And how that makes me a mole too.

## LESLIE GROLLMAN

*The Apple Tree*

The men carried flames on sticks; I remember how they made the stars disappear.

How they made the tree look strange against a dead sky.

•

Mama said *she's too young.*

*She needs to know what's what,* Daddy said. *She needs to know their place.*

I was five, I think it was, when they caught me kissing the boy who lived in the shack on the field. On his cheek, his left cheek, I remember because he had a scar on his right one and wouldn't let it be touched. Said it reminded him of the heat of a sun not from the sky.

*She needs to see what trees are for,* Daddy said.

*I'm not a baby anymore, Mama,* I wanted to say, but felt like I wanted to still be one then. Just for another hour, maybe. Just for the rest of that day.

Daddy dragged my arm almost off of me.

My shoes made skid marks, I remember, because one of them looked like that scar: like skin being pinched and pulled apart at the same time.

•

I wasn't allowed to say his name but I'll tell you. Harold. They gave him *Harold.*

He had another name none of them could say. Or wouldn't.

I could say it. Because he taught me.

He gave me a name, one that sounded like his real one. We would cup our little hands around each other's ears and feel our names. Like a summoning of anything bigger than we were.

•

The men carried flames on sticks; I remember how they made the stars disappear.

How they made the tree look strange against a dead sky.

How the sky felt mean.

How the faces of the men smelled meaner.

How their hateful breath fenced us in.

Harold's feet made skid marks too.

Our eyes connected how twigs make a nest.

We saw each other's eyes want something else as they lifted him to the tree.

We mouthed our secret names over and over.

We mouthed our names like drums asking the gods    *why.*

We mouthed our names like drums begging the gods   *help.*

His eyes went home to his Mama, to the place of his real name.

I swallowed his secret name over and over and over.

# LESLIE GROLLMAN

*Window Dressing*

Winded from my morning run
I stop to check my pulse at a storefront

A salad bowl frames my face: *what a rousing appetizer I would make*
Candlesticks for legs: *these hips would surely light some fire*

The momentary fog on the window erases my face
The blankness: a new page for a record of something
                                                    to be forgotten

I could make a gown from those curtains, like Scarlet did
Descend that staircase for my close-up with Mr. DeMille

But that dress would mean no more snacks and
JoanCrawfordComeFuckMePumps would surely break my ankles

I want to be barely-there, like a bas-relief
But the planets I read have something else in mind:
                                    the kind of wind the days bring

Betcha in that gown I could hitch a ride
in an egg carton, maybe for a song,
maybe

                    fly me to the Moon

## LESLIE GROLLMAN

*How to be an Asshole*

You butt in every Monday morning in the same coffee shop in the same barista's line just as your subordinate is about to order. You make a joke about raises and you are the only person laughing. You wink at the barista like she's in on it; you can't see disgust coming at you like a pie in a face at a carnival. You tell her *Mikey here'll get it* as you slap him on the left shoulder, hard, like you were slamming a door, the same place every time; you wouldn't notice a bruise there if his shirt was off. You stick your foot out in front of his just as he steps up to order. You gag laughing, not enough to choke yourself to death as Mike silently wishes you would. You turn to leave, see your new boss at the end of the line. She does not smile at you when you blow her a kiss. She looks through you. You tell your imaginary friend: *What a bitch!* You steamroll out the door yelling *Get outta my way, everybody is always in my way!* You do not see the crowd salute you: the chorus of middle fingers raised high in your name.

*Sleepwalking*

No way out, there is no way out. Among the ruins are the breakable, unbreakable, breakable pieces of me.

A flash grenade explodes.

*'There was a lamb,' said Grandma, opening her palms, gesturing at its fluffy wool by slightly rotating her wrists – puff – 'a lamb which didn't want to stay in the pen …' She drew the cigarette to her mouth again – puff. 'The little lamb gazed through the tiny hole of the wooden fence.'*

The flash is blinding. And I can't hear a thing.

*'She saw a different world outside the pen. An endless grassy field.'*

We are all running, running away. But we can't see a thing, we can't hear anything.

*'If she could get out of the fence, she would be free to graze on the grass field, free to run, free to bleat, free from the reign...'*

People are crashing into each other, stepping on each other, stacking over each other.

*'There was a flock of lambs …' Puff …*

Is this the stampede you were mentioning? This is twisted. This is really twisted. No way out, there is no way out.

*'The lambs were eaten by the Raptors.'*

Tear gas canisters explode.

We move backwards, pop open our umbrellas and crouch on the ground. Gun barrels are shooting at the shields of umbrellas. It is raining. We stand up and try to press forward. None of us know how much time is left in our lives. This could be our last day. I have written the sixth version of my last will. The bodies of the people in front of me are flickering, as if they are going to disappear at any moment. We move backwards, pop open our umbrellas and crouch on the ground. Gun barrels are shooting at us.

*Puff* ...

I am one of the protesters at the very front, being beaten up, arrested, locked away. I am the person throwing Molotov cocktails from behind. I am wailing. I am the first aider with the bleeding eye. I am the student with a broken helmet, lying on the ground. I am shivering. I am the reporter whose camera lens is cracked by a bullet. I am crawling, crawling with everyone to the way out, the way out.

*'... the little lamb didn't want to stay in the pen. She gazed and gazed through the tiny hole of the wooden fence. There lay the land of the free ...'*


The sleepwalkers crawl out of reeking sewers. It is dawn. Finally, there is no sign of the Raptors. No matter how cruel the world is, the sunrise is always gentle, Grandma said.

*The Arsonist and the Slouching Rain*

Oh, it's raining. It's raining again. Run, kids, run. The air is acidic and the ground is corrupted. Nobody is in love with the thunderstorm's loud crackling, the insidious rattling of the descending, stuttering rain. Relentless and ferocious, the rain of tumult is bashing and rampaging over the blossoming fields of vulnerable umbrellas; the rain of tumult is bending the stalk-like shafts; the rain of tumult misses no chance of slithering and slinking into the gap between two umbrella canopies, and sliding off the gores. The moisture and mist thus caress the skin, seeping deep into the pores, as they corrode and scald in scorn, leaving blood-red kisses of abrasions and rashes, invoking intense irritations and excruciating burning sensations.

There is no joy, no laughter, no singing or dancing in the rain. Go home, kids, go home. The rain is treacherous. The rain brings only tears. The heavy raindrops are trailing tongues of smoke and flames. The rain strikes your larynx and seizes you by the throat. The people under the umbrellas puke and choke. Vomitus mixes with painful tears. Stunned by the lynching, wheezing, they are overpowered by asphyxiation, incapacitated by paralysis, robbed entirely of perception. The rain is oppressive. The rain imprisons. The rain is death, because you did not listen.

The hymns are ceased. Terror is loosed upon the chanting of peace. The Raptors are coming. Fields of umbrellas disperse. White roses held by singers have fallen. Baton after baton lands on defenseless bodies. Bodies are captured, hand-cuffed, and thrust onto the ground with heavy blows and kicks to the head. Lost teeth, fractured ribs, one humerus is broken into three. Twisted slackened limbs clutch in streams of blood. Blood is dripping into pools of other people's blood. Hopeless yelling, desperate crying, moaning in despair, and endless mourning breaks out in sobbing;

wails of anguish, shrieks of fear are all deafeningly silent screaming, unanswered screaming; all perdure until they stop gasping in pain, lie down unconscious and scream their silent screams no more.

You stood in the mêlée of misery and fury, powerless, thinking it must be what music from hell sounds like. They told you that you deserve it. *If you disagree with us, you are a criminal, you are a rioter.* The shadows of tanks three decades ago cast indelible trauma on every soul. Tens of thousands of cold bodies scattered in the boulevards of the capital. In the past, the tragedy seemed so far away. Student protesters embraced and cried, as they do so now, but in another time and another place. In different dimensions, the gyre repeats itself. Now tanks manifest as white-clad thugs, waging undifferentiated attacks, wielding long knives and metal rods, conjuring the same cruel calamity.

*Help me!* But who to call when the police murder? Who rules when the police are part of the mob? The largest mob is waving their batons, brandishing their guns, placing their fingers steadily on the triggers. The beasts are unleashed, bullet after bullet. *Murdering, this is legal murdering.* The moment is frozen, engulfed by darkness. Did that just happen? Did police just shoot towards citizens they ought to be protecting? Her right eye is ruptured, his left eye is crying blood. Absolute power has guns, tear gas, water cannons, batons and pepper sprays of indiscriminate violence. The people only have helmets, goggles, masks and umbrellas. Yet the fiery eyes of fury cry no more. Final notes of will and testament are packed in his and her bags before they head to the streets. Why are they paying their youths and lives for the rights all humans are born with? The bullets and batons fall upon them. They start throwing bricks and stones, picking up rods and sticks.

With the fuse and lighter in your hands, you smell of gasoline. You stare at the smouldering barricades compiled of stacks of road signs, rubbish bins, wood planks, tyres and bicycles. You can barely take your eyes away from the flames. You are an arsonist, you are a criminal. Still we gather behind this burning barricade, with death on the other side, awaiting. We don't know each other's names. We are not cockroaches. We are not yellow objects. We are not corpses, not yet. We have names much more beautiful than rebels and rioters, because there are no rioters. There is only tyranny.

Oh, it's raining. It's raining canisters and canisters of tear gas again. The kids do not run. They cannot escape the fate of becoming dart boards made out of flesh. Black circles of scoring rings are imposed on their eyes, on their foreheads, on their chests. Each body part is an easy moving target. Each beating heart is a rhythm of unforgivable usurpation, inciting subversion of the great honourable state. The world snarls. When and where will it snap its menacing jaws? The prelude of massacre begins, in unison with the chiming passing-bells, as white mists of carcinogen mask their sights. The more it rains, the more the barricades burn.

WENDY LAW

*Dancing in the Dark*

He has arisen from the ashes. She is dancing in the dark. She doesn't know how high the sky is. He doesn't know how deep the earth is. The laser pointers, blue and green, are like stage lights, flinging as she is dancing in the dark.

The elders describe the student protesters with a Chinese proverb – 不知天高地厚 – 'unknowing of the tall sky and the deep earth'. The innocent and idealistic souls are like cattle trotting towards their tragic destiny.

*We gave our today, but how many tomorrows can we reclaim?*
*We gave our blood, we gave our lives, but what are we able to protect?*

She is dancing in the raging flames. Her hands are waving in blue gushes of water and white clouds of dust. Her legs are twisting and turning in the ruckus – *bam, boom, bang, pow* – bullets sear her clothes, rip her skin, scorch her waist and stomach; blood is trailing as the sound and fury are revolving around her. The wind is rising. Blasts are ringing in both of her ears. White mists are covering both of her eyes. Her legs are twisting, her arms are turning. His ashes are swivelling in the air. The wind has arisen as high as heaven, fallen as deep as the earth.

*The Hunt*

'I come from the north.'

The traveller's words were sharpened by an accent Shem had come to associate with heavily bearded nomads who wore no jewellery and had skin only slightly darker than goat's cheese. He'd seen it turn a painful shade of red within minutes of being exposed to the hot desert sun.

'The Plains were my home once and my people were of the desert, but the sun was cold there and the sand white.'

Shem's eyes darted around the circle as the nomad paused to take a sip of his ale. People of all sorts crowded around the bonfire, sitting on woven blankets or the bare stone of the square, standing, parents carrying their children to give them a better view. Shem even saw a couple of waifs scurry to the roof of a neighbouring building and lie down as they listened to the story, as if they were the most opulent of lords. Everyone's eyes were on the nomad's face, their expressions rapt.

'When I was eight cycles old, my father allowed me to join him on a hunt across the marshes in the Haerre mountain range. Few animals lived near our village, but the mountains were teeming with wildlife.'

Shem felt a grin bloom on his face as he leaned forward in anticipation. Hunting stories were his favourite. They were always so full of adventure and travelling and creatures that couldn't possibly truly exist – which is exactly what Shem would've said mere hours ago about the animal splayed at the nomad's feet. For the thousandth time that evening, he glanced at the magnificent feline, its smoky coat blotted with black and steel-grey spots gleaming in the light of the flames. If not for its size, Shem would've claimed it was a cat. But how could it be, when its head almost reached the nomad's hipline when standing? Besides, none of the strays that ran around his city had a pattern even remotely similar to this one – the way the large spots followed one another almost reminded him of snake scales.

Shem thought glumly of the wasteland that surrounded his own city. It was situated in the middle of the continent's hottest desert and therefore almost barren as far as wildlife was concerned. Oh, there were plenty of lizards and scorpions and such, but Shem found the smaller fauna exceptionally boring.

The animal lifted its head lazily and blinked at its master, its tail twitching with a steady rhythm. Shem remembered seeing it earlier that day as he stared in awe at the caravan entering the city. He and his friends had combed through the crowds gathered around numerous bonfires that burned in the squares that night, looking for the feline and its owner. They were easy enough to spot, but relatively hard to locate amongst the hundreds of visitors that had recently congregated in the Alliance.

The nomad placed a hand on the animal's head, giving it a pat similar to those Shem often gave the strays that passed his way. The feline closed its amber eyes and purred in satisfaction.

'Her name is Tawa. I found her eight days into the hunt. She was bleeding, an arrow stuck in her shoulder. Probably an awkward shot.' The traveller moved his fingers to her left shoulder and pushed aside some of her fur to show off the scar hidden beneath. Tawa jerked, but otherwise remained calm.

'How did you get near her? Didn't she attack you?' Shem blurted out, remembering too late that it was considered impolite to interrupt the nomads' tales. The boy sitting on Shem's left side elbowed him with a pointed look.

The traveller's green eyes were ringed with a thick black line and had an intensity to them that made Shem squirm when they focused on him. The man smiled, evidently not disturbed by Shem's interjection. His white teeth, surrounded by a shaggy jet-black beard, reminded Shem of the moon in the dark night sky. 'She did, but she was too weak to cause any real damage.'

Tawa's ears twitched and turned as different sounds drew her attention, but her amber eyes stayed still, focused on her master, communicating a sense of calm that Shem found odd in a creature of her wild nature.

'I caught her, earning myself an earful from my father.' The nomad chuckled. 'I took out the arrow and nursed her back to health. When she was ready to strike out on her own again, we went back to the mountains and I released her. She sniffed around for a while, then padded over to lie at my feet. We've been together since.'

There were a few gasps of admiration from the crowd, people still staring at Tawa with large eyes, half of the crowd starting every time she moved, as if afraid she would attack.

'We thank you for your tale, nomad,' said someone, several murmurs echoing the words. The bearded traveller nodded solemnly, pulling a pipe from his pocket as people started to disperse, most of them keeping what they considered a safe distance between themselves and Tawa. Shem heard excited conversations spark up as they left, wondering what other strange tales they might hear around the city that night. The traveller paid them no mind and searched the many pockets of his layered garments until he found a pouch of herbs. Soon Shem, the nomad and Tawa were the only ones left sitting at the bonfire.

'What's your name, boy?'

Shocked that the man had addressed him, Shem stuttered a little. 'Shem, nomad.' The customary title for those who lived or travelled with caravans slid off his tongue without thought.

'My name is Ilai.' The man bowed his head the way northmen always did, slightly to the side as if their necks couldn't bend forward. Shem did his best to imitate it, but he caught a shade of a smirk on Ilai's face when he looked up and knew he must not have done it right.

'Have you travelled at all, Shem? Do you know the places I spoke of?' Ilai asked, stuffing his pipe with practiced movements.

Shem shook his head, wishing he could have nodded instead. 'No. I've lived in Raegis Alliance all my life.'

'I see. Do you wish to stay here? Or do you want more?'

Shem hesitated, struggling to lay bare his dreams. He'd nursed them all his life, striving to make them strong enough to push him through what lay ahead, and yet the thought of voicing them aloud made him fear they would be blown away like sand on the desert wind. He wanted a bed to sleep in, to own a fresh change of clothes, for people to take note of him as he passed. He wanted to visit the incredible places nomads described, climb the mountains, smell the sea. When he looked at Ilai, however, he saw his thoughts already mirrored in the traveller's eyes and knew there was no need to put them into words. 'I want more.'

The nomad's smile grew and he puffed on his pipe contentedly. 'Then travel.'

A sweet smell reached Shem's nostrils, making him wonder what kind of herbs the nomad was smoking. He wasn't sure if Ilai was mocking him – after all, he was a street urchin and travelling cost coin. But the look in the traveller's eyes was kind, not sardonic. 'I have no means to travel, nomad.'

The dark green eyes scrutinised him silently until Shem shifted, suddenly uncomfortable. He felt as if the nomad wasn't just looking *at* him, but *into* him. His eyes had glazed over and though Shem saw Ilai sitting right across from him, he had a strange feeling the man was far away. Finally, when his pipe went out, the nomad shuddered, shaking his head as if to clear it. He dumped the remainder of the herbs into the fire. The flames surged up, their colour intensifying from orange to a deep red before changing back after a moment and continuing to crackle merrily.

Shem stared, left speechless by the astonishing phenomenon, while Ilai calmly put away his pipe and stood up. Tawa was on her feet in a blink, jumping out of her master's way gracefully as he stepped around the upturned crate he'd been sitting on. Shem finally looked up, wondering if he had simply imagined the whole thing, when Ilai paused to glance back, a smile in his eyes.

'Worry not, Shem of Raegis. You will saunter through the grandest of palaces and trudge through the foulest of moors. You will bear witness to greatness. The next time our paths cross, my eyes will not know you, but Tawa never forgets a friendly face. Until then, may light shine upon your path and may your aim be ever true. Farewell.'

The nomad left, shadowed by the magnificent animal that trailed him on soft paws, leaving Shem to stare after them, confused and filled with burning hope.

# THOMAS CARROLL

*Just One Second*

'What about this black hole at the middle of the galaxy?'

In the corner of the cafe the TV was playing the news on mute, showing the new picture of a burning orange eye, and the dark hole at its centre. Benjamin was watching it as he and his husband, Matthew, were eating breakfast.

Matthew sighed quietly. 'What about it?' he said.

'Well, it's just there, right. Sucking everything up. Sucking us up right now.'

Matthew put down the menu. 'Do you want something to eat?'

'It's just there – no, I'm fine,' Benjamin said, shaking his head. His eyes quickly returned to the TV. 'It's just there, the black hole, you know? Right now. Doing that. It's out there and we could actually be there and see it.'

The waitress came round with more coffee. It smelt burnt. Matthew accepted it with a smile; Benjamin didn't notice his cup being filled.

'Yeah, but it's far. And you can't actually see it,' Matthew said. He'd tried explaining this two days ago too. 'You just know it's there because of how it affects things around it. That image is special, or something. It took them ages.'

'No, well. You know what I mean,' Benjamin said. He toyed with his coffee cup for a moment, glancing back at the TV. His mouth worked on something, and his brow held a frown. 'And I mean, that's just one of them – galaxies. There's so many more. So there's so many more black holes and stars and planets. There's like millions and millions of galaxies and –'

'And they all have millions of stars,' Matthew finished for him.

'And they all have millions of stars, yeah. And those planets, and all that. Forever. Just so much.'

Matthew shrugged. 'I don't think about it.'

'I do. I can't stop thinking about it,' Benjamin said, staring at the plastic table-cover now. 'Just all that out there. And us just sitting here in this place. And there's that black hole and there's suns and planets, and there might even be something talking about it like us, sitting on their own planet and talking about it.'

'Could be,' Matthew said. His eyes were drawn outside.

'And that's just it. Everything is happening. Everything is happening somewhere, right this second. Right here on Earth even. People are being born.' Benjamin glanced up to see if anyone was close, but the booths nearest to them were empty. He lowered his voice anyway. 'And being killed and fucking and laughing and crying and having the best day of their life and having the worst day of life. Right this second.' Benjamin rubbed his hands up his forearms, like he did whenever he was nervous. 'Right as we're sitting here drinking our coffee.'

Matthew nodded slowly. He had nothing to say. Benjamin had been fixed on this all week; his eyes were dark and heavy.

'I'm sorry,' Benjamin said. 'Sorry if you don't like me saying that. I just can't stop thinking about it, you know? It's just all around us, all the time.'

'It's fine.'

'I'm sorry.'

They sat in silence. Benjamin fiddled with his coffee cup. The door jingled abruptly as two new customers came in. They sat down behind Benjamin and Matthew, and called for the waitress. They seemed happy.

'I just can't get it out of my head,' Benjamin began again, once the people were done ordering. His voice was softer now, almost defeated. His finger ran along a crease in the table-cover. 'I find myself thinking about it all the time. At night. It's hard to sleep.'

'I've been worrying about you.'

'I know, I'm okay. I'm okay. It's just ... all that I was talking about; what we were saying about the stars and the galaxies and everything here happening on Earth? That's just one second. But then there's another second. And another, and it just goes on and on and we only live what, eighty years, maybe?'

'Hopefully.'

'So then it just goes on without us too. Just on and on forever, because who's going to stop it, right? Nobody. And we'll be gone and all these things that we'll never see are going to happen for millions and millions of years.' Benjamin's hand pressed white against the table. 'They're going to happen for eternity.'

Matthew watched him in distress. 'Let's just go do something?' he said, after a moment.

Benjamin breathed in hard. The silence spread between them. A customer at the counter asked the waitress a question, and the TV channel was changed to something else.

Finally Benjamin said, 'Okay.'

# KIT NICHOLSON

*Jam*

On the night Phillips died I knew, for sure, that I would survive.

He'd gone to join Tibbs and Moore and Grainger and Davison and Yates and Higgins and Smith and Sergeant Stock and Captain Rivers. And mother and Rebecca and Aunt Ruth and Pop. And Patch and Bubbles and Mr Tom. And Bertie.

They'd snatched his life away. Phillips, who'd shared his mother's jam with the men, spooned grotesquely on two grimy fingers into our gaping mouths; who'd shouted crossword puzzle clues, unanswered; who'd howled with a whooping laugh; who'd mastered an uncanny impression of Major Forsyth. They'd killed him. They'd stolen his future. They'd silenced his voice. They'd set him free.

He had been the last of us. Everyone around me now stood in the boots of the dead or wounded. My friends who had been filled with such hope, who had played football behind the line, whose lives brimmed with enthusiasm, spilling over in laughter. A few now lay quiet, hollow under coarse white sheets, mere spectres of their old selves. But most had been laid to rest forever under the heavy comfort of foreign mud. The lucky ones.

And here I stood, blood warming my icy veins, the most ghostly of the lot. Left behind to walk the earth, to traipse through hungry mud, alone. Left to continue the fight for something far beyond my understanding, beyond anyone's. I was empty. Numb. Stunned. I didn't care. I had nothing to care for. I was the perfect soldier; I accepted Death; I welcomed it. But I was invincible. Reluctantly, inevitably, bitterly invincible. This war would not kill me. Spanish flu would not kill me. Cigarettes and alcohol, not even grief would eventually kill me. I would be made to wait. A whole lifetime.

Not Bertie. That firecracker of orange hair and dirty freckles. He was my best friend, my confidant, my comrade. Only two years had separated us, but he'd got stuck. I'd kept getting older, but he stayed six years old. Small boys fight, we all know that. Our temperatures ran high, breathless, our stringy little bodies swollen and contorted with passion and energy. We never felt anything that wasn't on a grand scale, explosive, exciting, dangerous.

Brain bleed, they called it. He hit his head on the toy box and never woke up. I didn't mean to kick so hard, both feet and burning with frustration. I can still feel what it felt like, hear the ringing in my ears, the tension in my neck and shoulders. But I don't remember why.

Mother had got sick then. Father too, though his was self-inflicted.

And now Phillips.

They'd got him in the face, ripped his jaw wide open, chunks of flesh like sticky jam. He'd never laugh again but he didn't know it. I did. I'd carry that silence with me forever.

## KATHERINE O'CONNELL

*After*

Cora could reach the roof through Fallon's window. She could tighten her laces, hike up her jeans, kick one leg through the open frame, and hoist herself along the fire escape. Up there, she could see everything: the Empire State Building, lit this time of year with purple and white for the graduates from New York University; the cursed JMZ train, standing room only, no matter the hour; the snake of brake-lights choking the Williamsburg Bridge, the blaring of horns audible all the way in Bushwick.

As she drummed her fingers on the grimy glass, Cora could recall sneaking up there with Seamus when they were little. After their parents had gone to sleep, they would venture out to lie on their backs and count the stars, searching for the wishbone constellation their mother promised they had been born under. They were only kids then, stifling yawns behind closed palms and refusing to admit they could hardly keep their eyes open.

Legally, they were still kids. It would be two months before Cora could buy cigarettes (not that she would) or Seamus could rent porn (he absolutely would) but they had grown up overnight, their lives now firmly divided into "before" and "after." So far, "after" looked like Seamus staying in his room all day, skipping out on the first day of junior finals while Cora made a showing for the both of them. With her uniform necktie fastened such that it bordered strangulation, the looks Cora drew in the school hallway had been worse than if she had shown up naked, her most frequent nightmare come to life.

That morning, the students had watched as their school president checked the batteries in her calculator and sharpened two pencils before the calculus test. When they thought she was not looking, they had whispered her name, deep into each other's ears. Already, they had known everything.

Without question, Seamus's teachers had excused him for the rest of term. He was getting straight A's already. Cora's younger sister was not so lucky. Fallon's teachers had reverted to pass/fail, but that she rarely showed up meant she would likely have to repeat all classes. It might have been embarrassing, had she known the name of a single person in her grade. Fallon ran with an older crowd, dropouts from the university who smoked weed in Washington Square and were on secret listservs for all the best bacchanals in the city. At sixteen, she was always heading to some rave in Queens or warehouse party on the Lower East Side. Fallon was exactly like their mother in that way, forever intent on living life headfirst.

Cora could reach the roof through Fallon's window, but while she had been at school that day, solving for X and finding slope, her father had paid someone to paint it shut. Cora's sister had surely put up a fight, which was why she was gone now, along with her backpack and best pair of Chuck Taylors. It would be a week before she came home. Maybe two.

Running her fingers along the viscid sill, Cora wondered how long it would take their father to notice Fallon was missing. She was seldom home and he worked long hours. After last night, Cora doubted he would ever set foot in Fallon's room again, what with her fifth-floor window being the one their mother had thrown herself from before dinner.

The aunts had arrived around eight, the older packing Bisquick and the younger touting whipped cream and M&M's. Cora's father had called them, soliciting distraction while he and the EMTs got the body to the nearest hospital. And it was a body then. Already. That couldn't have been their mother.

Without her perched in her usual chair at one end of the table, it fell to Cora to keep lactose-intolerant Seamus away from the whipped cream nozzle and little Derry, all of eleven months, from swallowing M&M's. Yes, Cora had always wanted to be someone's mom, but not like this. She had a math test to study for.

Dragging her hand away from the window ledge, the faintest hint of white sticking to her prints, Cora glanced outside. It was getting dark again. The first full day of "after" was nearly through. That probably should have meant something, but Cora's mind was elsewhere, fixated on the string of numbers burrowing deeper and deeper like a tick in her brain.

She had spent too long on the first half of the test and run out of time, so in a panic, for the last question, she had scrawled "13," which could well have been right, but would lose her points for a lack of work demonstrated. Had Seamus been there, she could have copied. He always knew the answer.

As she turned from the window, stocking-clad feet scraping along Fallon's flea-market rug, it occurred to her that they had no intention of actually grading her exam. The nuns would pardon her as they had her brother. Awesome. That would come back to bite her when she and Katie Chen were neck-and-neck in the race for valedictorian.

"Hey, Seamus?" Cora called, desperate for the answer. "I need you to solve an equation for me." She barreled into his room next door, but on turning the light, found her brother's bed made, the ever-glowing screen of his laptop pitch dark. "Seamus?" It was not like him to go off without telling her. "Where are you?"

She poked her head into her own room, empty, and suddenly felt her heart-rate begin to elevate. Her brother was staying home today. That was what he had told her when she knocked on his door at 7:30 that morning, his uniform blazer tucked over her arm, that hideous red tie folded into the pocket. He didn't go to school because he was staying at home today. He was supposed to be staying at home today.

"Seamus, answer me."

Cora threw open the bathroom door next, then her parents' room, and the linen closet. He wasn't there. He was supposed to be here, but he was gone. He was nowhere. He was just fucking nowhere.

"I swear to God, Seamus, if you—"

"...see that one up there? That's Capricorn. That's Daddy's. Kinda looks like a triangle."

Whipping her head around, Cora peered through the slats in the paneling of the open linen closet door. Derry's room, one over, was ajar, the overhead doused, dim yellow light spilling into the hall.

"That one over there," her brother's soft tenor continued, "that's the one Fallon was born under. Technically Libra, but, like Mommy always says, 'That girl will sting you worse than a scorpion.'"

Inching forward, Cora placed her fingertips on Derry's door and pushed, staining the warm chestnut wood with five smears of paint. That's how many there were now. Their whole family could be counted on one hand.

"Oh, look who it is," Seamus greeted her. "Another water sign." They were lying on their backs in there, Seamus with his head propped against Derry's crib, Derry curled into the crook of his older brother's left arm. "Come join us."

Cora stepped into the room, a linen closet in and of itself, and drew her eyes skyward. The ceiling of Derry's room was freshly peppered with stars, tacked onto the ceiling with blobs of tape to form small-scale constellations. Cora recognized the one she and her twin used to look for back by the window.

"I was just telling Derry how Mom used to let us go up on the roof and look at the stars when we were little." Seamus raised his arm over Derry's head and pointed above the door, where their little brother's sign crept down onto the wall. "That's Gemini, right? It's huge. It barely fit."

Biting down on the inside of her cheek, Cora blinked back the sting beginning to form behind her eyes. "When did you do this?"

"Earlier." Seamus kept his eyes on the sky. "Dad was waiting for the painter, so, you know, he was here to watch Derry, and I mostly just wanted to get out of the house and do something."

Cora exhaled, her heart-rate finally starting to steady. "Seamus, Mom didn't let us go up there. We had to sneak out."

"No way," her brother snorted. "When we first moved in, she hacked away at that window for hours with an X-Acto. Don't you remember? The people who lived here before us had it sealed, but she wanted fresh air, and the night sky at her fingers."

Cora stood on her tiptoes to reach the ordered stars of Derry's sign. "I don't remember," she confessed, fingertips hovering over the plastic. "Derry won't remember her at all."

"He might."

"Seamus, what are we supposed to tell him when he asks where she's gone?"

"The truth." He patted their little brother's mop of red hair. "Mom's gone out the window. She wanted to try and count the stars."

# ANTHI CHEIMARIOU

## *viola*

*If music be the food of love, play on*

A pitted stave and a bowed instrument
Doubles of melody repeated or lost,
Inner voices in the alto clef
Outer voices in the treble clef.

*Give me excess of it, that, surfeiting,*

Follow the knight-errant.
Schönberg will not be disappointed.
Perfect fifth and the world becomes
Festive, Chloe is seen dancing in a field.

*The appetite may sicken, and so die.*

Embrowned with silver strings
It can lie bleeding in the sound of love
Vibrating by the force of the wind

*O, it came o'er my ear like the sweet sound,*

Flowers clashing together,
A hidden rainbow of sounds.
Try to measure their colour in a chromatic
Scale – you will be left with only one.

*That breathes upon a bank of violets*

Purple the colour... of love?
Violets crashed, a bank of clouds
And identities bound.
Viola would laugh in a coda with dominant sevens.

## ANTHI CHEIMARIOU

---

*Do I Really?*

The Boy says and kisses The Girl
'I do! I do!'

Shadowless room, movement detected
faces erased, intoxicated. Careful step, falsetto tone

calling for a round, in this empty room.

He appears like fungus in the air she is breathing;
the world spins and for now...

Is it really? Is it though? Only for now?

Clinging sound of frozen $H_2O$
turned pink and hollow.

Pink becoming green
is the beginning of my original sin.

Never touching lips
the threshold you cross
with the 'I do'.

Crooked blue necktie
A lonely grey one and a smile

You always choose

You            I do

## ANTHI CHEIMARIOU

*Buried Heart*


Circling a black spot
Out in the sky
Black clouds crying down

Black feathers fluttering aloud

Red beak
Becoming blue
And black

Loud shots, and the raven loses sight

Hears only the
Pumping blood
Of a dying heart;

It closes its eyes and breathes

Wind whooshes the
Black spot in the sky
Away from the killer's eye

This is the naked land of crystalized fluids

The land comes closer
And the two
Will become one with the clouds as witnesses

The raven at last     lies dead     next to his buried heart

*Day*

The beginning of a person is the beginning of the world. There are sounds, dapples of changing colour. Vast rooms of nausea and confusion. Too much movement. The world outside is one long street. In the days after the beginning of this disgusting world, there are animals; not proper animals, mind – only cats and dogs. Eventually the rooms become smaller.

We live in closed worlds. I don't know anything about your world and you don't know anything about mine. But some things remain the same, like blue and pink and grey skies; worms in the soil, birds in the trees. In my world, right now, I look up at the small circular window in the ceiling. Outside, a damp evening in November. I see the clouds. Winter is deepening, its soul ripening and growing round.

I'd cut through the backroads and large gardens of plush greens and radiant colours to get home quickly. The grey afternoon sky overhead presaged more snow, but the gardens were bathed with fragrant breezes, and the soft turf beneath my feet was redolent with creeping thyme and coriander.

'I'm home,' I'd said through the door when I arrived home. 'It's me. I'm home.'

Now I listen to her crying through the bathroom door, her whispers nothing more than nonsensical mumblings; soon I can hardly catch more than hisses of her breath. It hurts – there are no other words for it.

I take a deep breath; around me the flat smells of lager mingled with smoke and cheap liquor. Alcohol, tobacco and stale misery pour into my mouth; the scents intertwine but never resolve into a single perfume. The couple upstairs begin to argue as I sit outside the bathroom. One shout is followed by another, followed by another, until a throb of angry voices drowns out the sounds of my mother's grief.

Somewhere below me, a phone begins to ring.

I put my mouth to the crack in the door. 'That phone,' I say, my voice muffled through the wood. 'It's going off again.'

In the bathroom there's rustling, and after a moment she opens the door, looking quite calm with a glass of cheap red wine in one hand. But the more I look, the more a great weariness seems to seep from her, an air of uncertainty. Taut lines mar her face, and the ragged bandage binding her other hand looks fragile where she cradles it against her chest. Swaying on her feet, she opens her mouth as if to say something but thinks better of it.

The door upstairs slams again. We wince.

'How are you?' I ask.

Long seconds trickle by, carrying with them the rustling of the trees outside, the howl of the wind through the streets, a distant clap of thunder.

'How are you?' I ask again.

This time she turns to look at me. She is composed of many elements, of charm and charisma and intelligence; and of firmness, even aggression. This contradiction in her nature is maddening.

Her face is perfectly still. She says, 'Thank you for asking.' And turns away.

Exhausted though I am, sleep is neither peaceful nor easy, and I battle my way through a parade of uneasy dreams. Fragmented glimpses of the last few weeks – scraps of speech, faces of no consequence speaking words I can't understand. Dreams of hospital doors and muttered apologies and a bright, stabbing sorrow so haunting I shudder awake several times, only to find the details of the dreams scuttling away.

When morning comes I dress for school, quietly slipping out the door so as not to wake her, tucking the shopping list I've written into the pocket of my skirt. Outside the air is frigid and tight. The estate is quiet at this hour; I hear nothing but the wind stirring through the birches and willows that surround our building. I pass the old tennis court and the empty, rusted swimming pool, decorated now by vines and weeds and untameable flowers; the grass around the buildings is now so long it's like wading through dense, muddy water. Likely it's been many years since anybody cared to tend to this place.

When I get to school I smoke a cigarette in the toilets. Despite the rules and restrictions of school, I do whatever I want and it feels good. I smoke, I drink. The speed of it all, the emotional overload, and the pain every now and then dulls my brain, numbs my perceptual apparatus.

I know I can't change the shit I live in so I try to change myself.

The day drifts by slowly. Icy winds seep through cracks in the windows and sigh through the corridors, carrying with them the sweet sense of snow to come.

I do no work and make no attempt to; the teachers say nothing. I say nothing. I can go whole days without speaking sometimes.

By the time I leave it's snowing in earnest; heavy flakes deaden all sound. Every surface soon becomes outlined in white, the ground underneath me a mass of slush. Breathing the fresh air deeply, I walk the three kilometres to the Rema 1000 in Norheim, approaching the building in a daze, only distantly aware of the flow of people around me.

I take what we need. I've got it down to a fine art.

The walk back is longer, harsher. It's bitterly cold out, and long crystals of frost sit on everything around me. Overhead, clouds rib the hazy sky. Besides the birds taking refuge on the high branches, everything is perfectly still, like the dreary weather has stripped all life from the land. The street lamps are on by the time I arrive home; the small clouds of misty, milky light serve to make everything appear darker. The shadows between trees and buildings seem deeper than if there was no light at all.

She's in the kitchen when I let myself in.

'Hello,' I say, but don't expect an answer. She looks better today, stronger. She doesn't reply but that's okay. The colour in her cheeks is enough. When I look at her I think, hard. Let myself analyse her quietly, from the circles under her eyes to the fingers that tremble underneath every surface she touches. Her eyes, the eyes that flicker from object to object, never settling on any one thing at any one time.

I think that it's so very hard, sometimes, to admit to ourselves that we're lonely – it's easier, I think, to invent something to buy into.

I put the groceries in the cupboards, throwing myself into it. Organise everything like I'm being paid for it. Let the cupboard door swing closed when I'm done. She's lingering in the doorway, tired and drained.

She opens her mouth to say something, to offer a word or two, but nothing comes out.

She has nothing to say.

# HARRISON MACLEOD-BONNAR

*McCartney and I*

There are quiet moments, when a freshly lit cigarette glows between my fingers and the wind curves by the open car window, that the past comes back to me unannounced through the speaker of my transistor radio and I reach for that Polaroid photograph of a crying girl with no name. She has a name, of course. She may even have told me it. I have forgotten it now.

Only at these moments, when there is nothing but empty road and music for memories, do I find myself thinking of her again. It takes me by surprise, as always, and forces me to pull over, send the wilting ash soaring out the window, withdraw that photograph, and listen.

Its edges are creased, sheathed carefully between cash notes, receipts, cinema tickets, a family portrait. There is something that keeps it between forefinger and thumb and saves it from life's waste bin. I am there also. Both of us, faces in the past. There is a cruel brightness in our expressions, like the glint of the reflecting sun on the photograph film, that makes it difficult to look at even now.

There is no mistaking those chords and the melody that carries this nameless girl on its offbeat rhythm. I know it well. One chord and the space between us dissolves, thin as the sheaf of folded worthless papers that line my wallet.

It begins, I think, with rejection, a false moustache and a bad haircut from 1961.

Her idle loneliness announces itself; it maroons her there in a darkened room crackling with laughter and music. My friend, dressed as Albert Camus, is hosting a party for the New Year. His jacket collar is raised and his hair is one hard slick. A limp cigarette is softening on the bridge of his lip. He keeps a paperback copy nearby with the author photograph to show people the resemblance.

'I told you no one would get it,' I say.

'It's unusual though. A good conversation starter, you know.' He winks. 'Another?' He swings an empty green beer bottle by the neck.

Before I can answer he vanishes into the kitchen and returns with a bottle in each hand and one cooling under his arm.

'Cheers.' We lean against a table glistening with puddles of spilt alcohol.

'Doesn't it bother you? All these strangers touching your stuff, drinking your booze, ruining your furniture.'

He takes a long meditative sip and weighs my question.

'Nah.'

'Do you actually know everyone here?'

'Not really. All are welcome, you know.' I envy his smiling good-natured openness, the host seldom without an offering under his arm, that disgraces my quiet cynicism.

'Alright.' I survey the room. I almost miss her between the shifting wall of bodies dancing over a stained carpet. Two girls lean for pause against the cracked wallpaper next to her, reaching and clicking lighters, fogging the flat windows with short exasperated breaths and ignoring her.

'Who's that then?' I point with the tip of the bottle, still cold from the fridge.

'Who?' Camus asks.

'That girl.'

She is straight collar-length hair, a bold fringe and a cobalt-blue blazer. Her brogues are scraped at the toe and furnished with untied laces. She studies them now, sitting in a chair against the wall. She has brushed the corners of her false moustache with eye liner. I know because I can see the watery streaks running from her eyes turning black at the corners of her mouth like warpaint. It's peeling at the corners. Her foot taps maniacally offbeat. She is dressed as late-sixties Paul McCartney, as am I.

'No idea.' Another sip. 'Oh, I think that's his date.' Camus turns his head and points at our friend dressed as Steve McQueen, slurring through a story with a leather jacket arm draped over a girl resembling Marilyn Monroe, and tilts my borrowed shades down the bridge of his nose.

'Did he not introduce her?' I ask.

'Nah.'

'She's crying … We should do something.'

'Like what? What are you going to do?' Camus laughs.

'*Something*. It's depressing.'

Camus has already left and is instead holding up the photograph of the real Albert Camus to a girl dressed impressively as the seventies incarnation of David Bowie, widening her eyes in feigned interest, who will later become his first wife.

I can tell, minute by minute, a small piece of McCartney-girl is leaving. It rises and steps away quietly so that the marks on her shoes fade with distance. It brushes past unapologetically and glides between the gaps between bodies. It turns the front door handle behind her. It descends the stairwell steps and wanders onto the street, blinking and removing her shoes. It's late; she won't check the roads before crossing when it's this quiet. A small act of anarchy. Minute by minute, a small piece of her leaves until there is more of her outside in the cold than here with me. Not really with me, only near me.

Giving up on Camus, I lower myself into a nearby chair and take a final cursory sip of beer, as if merely for quiet repose. She's done a better job of it than me. Period accuracy yet a hint of flair. Somewhere between *Revolver* and *The White Album*. It almost merits a passing remark. I look down at my own modest cable-knit sweater over a white Henley shirt.

*Nice moustache. It's as if we've coordinated.*

*You like the Beatles?*

*I like your moustache. I grew mine myself.*

Around her neck a handkerchief hangs in half-Windsor exhaustion. She vanishes behind two friends convening on the radiator between us with bent elbows and lip-marked glasses hovering just below the chin. We wait like passengers on a platform for a train that will never come. When the friends leave, I lean slightly in the chair so that an immutable creak cuts the air.

'Don't talk to me,' she says.

'Jesus. I wasn't going to.' I raise my hands in surrender.

'Yes, you were. I saw you walk over here. If you've come to humiliate me don't bother.'

'Why would I do that?'

'You're friends.' She moves her eyes towards McQueen.

'That guy? Barely know him.' McQueen and I are childhood friends. In the years to come, I will become the godfather to his children.

'Lucky you.'

James Dean, with a Polaroid camera hanging over one shoulder by a black strap, walks by and without warning clicks and drowns our corner in instantaneous searing light, immortalising this moment in dispensable film. Two white, moustached faces, a half-empty bottle of beer in my hand and a girl with dried tears on her cheeks.

Dean hands me the picture and walks away. I look at it for the first time in my life. When we were but slow-burning white corners yet to be fully rendered.

'What do you think?' I ask, as if I took it myself.

She fakes a smile.

'You're quite good at that, pretending to be happy.'

'You've only just met me.'

'True.'

In the far corner someone slides one of Camus' precious records out of its sleeve and onto the turntable. A Lennon B-side lulls the room.

'Do you know this one?' I ask.

'Of course.'

'Lennon's better at being sad, I think.' I pause, lower my head and look again at the Polaroid. 'I think it's about a man in love with a girl he doesn't want to love.'

'He's trying to leave her. Over and over.'

'She promises the earth to him and he believes her. That's the worst part, that he believes her. He stays with her, this man, but he doesn't really know why. Not your average pop song.'

'I prefer those ones anyway.'

We exchange a fleeting smile. I offer her the photograph.

She raises a hand smudged with black tears. 'Keep it.'

•

The song on the radio dies gracefully and it ends, as it always does, with that photograph between my fingers, the slow turn of the volume dial, and images of her leaving, as she does each time I revisit Camus' living room, with a false departing smile and a moustache stolen from Paul McCartney falling from her lips.

*Surgery*

I look down at her heart, still beating in my hands. Droplets of blood slip through the crevices in my palms and trail down onto my forearms. There's still life pumping through it, expanding and collapsing like the chest of a premature baby in an incubator.

'Can I have that back, please?' she asks me.

She's sat on a wooden stool beside me. There's a gaping hole in her chest from where I have gouged out the organ. The blood that had been pumping through her is pouring out, soaking her skin and clumping the ends of her long hair together. Against the deep red stains on her chest, she is white. Her eyes bore into me and I cannot help but look away.

The heart in my hands is getting weaker, struggling to reach its previous size with every new breath it takes. I can almost hear it wheezing, trying to draw in oxygen like a ninety-year-old man with lung cancer.

'Please,' she says, her voice little more than a whisper now.

My hands clasp tighter around the part of her which is mine now. As I clench, the last droplets of blood filter through the arteries, squeezing onto the floor. It has stopped moving, and is beginning to turn black.

I examine it, impressed at my almost perfect extraction. My nails have cut neatly through her tendons and there are no major tears. It sits limp in my hands and I wait for it to fully dehydrate. This is my favourite part of the process – watching the shape of someone else condense into a dark, heavy stone in my palms.

She has stopped breathing now. She no longer has the strength to support herself and is draped over the stool in an upside-down U shape. The arch of her pelvis up from the floor makes her look like a gymnast. Her head is against the stone; there is a sense of knowing in her eyes. If they weren't hazed by the mist of death, I would wonder if she was looking right into my soul.

We sit like this for a while; her body to the side of me – a convex supported by the stool she had been perched on – and her heart cooling in my hands. Her blood is hardening onto my skin. It has trouble sticking to me; I blow at it and the flakes lift into the air. They flutter like confetti, settling either on the table in front of me, or dropping closer to the ground and landing on the skin that should have protected her.

When her heart is no bigger than a prune, I drop it onto the table. It bounces. I inspect it more closely – it should have shattered on collision. All the others usually do. I try again, holding it slightly higher this time. Again, it bounces, as if it is made of rubber.

Her arms suddenly drop. They had been resting on her stomach, but now they are splayed on the floor. She has made a cross with herself: her ankles neatly placed over one another, her arms outstretched. The stool is the only interruption in the crucifix her body seems to be trying to form.

I stretch for the heart which has bounced just outside my reach, recalling how to revive it from the depths of my memory. Rolling it between my palms, I warm it. I lift it to my lips and breathe air into it. The heart expands, then quickly collapses again. A cracking sound fills the space. I repeat the blowing and watch as her head lifts slightly from the floor, then claps onto it again.

The tips of my fingers tingle as I look around. On the far side of the room is the box I prepared for this potential rare, unexpected occasion. It scrapes along the table as I position it. Fumbling around for a needle and thread with one hand, I keep rolling the heart against me with the other. Lightning bolts of pink start to reinvigorate it. I suck the end of the thread and focus on keeping myself steady as I push it through the eye of the needle. Once through, I place it on the table and shake the tension out of my arms.

My boots make dull thuds as I walk around the workroom. It doesn't take me long to gather the things I need; a white sheet to place her on and the tissue to stuff into any empty spaces. The fabric whips through the air and lands over an empty space on the cool floor. I scoop up her body and lay her carefully onto the floor.

I pick up the needle and jam it into my finger. It pushes through my skin easily and I let the droplets of blood fall onto the heart which lies between her body and mine. It swells, hydrating itself with the parts of me that I am willing to give to her. It grows and grows, until the valves are large enough for me to see them start opening and closing.

I place the heart back between her breasts and begin to sew. Yet again I thank myself for the immaculate extraction – it makes it easy for me to put her back together again. The thread soon disintegrates into her flesh. I continue to bleed over her, until she regains the pink flush she had before. The blood rushing through her veins echoes around the room. I neatly knot the end of the thread.

I stuff the tissue into the hole and bandage the area. Her breathing is short and shallow, but her eyes unglaze. They flit around the room before focussing on me. I lean over her to prevent her from straining herself to see me more clearly.

'We are a part of each other now,' I say.

'Thank you,' she says.

I lower my body down towards her and press my lips to hers. They are cold, so I hold myself there until I can feel the final inches of her body being warmed by mine.

## DAWN BRATHWAITE

*Fear of the High-Rise*

I cover myself with vertical blinds afraid,
fearing those eyes of the high-rise
so many of them          out     and
            inside
as if watching and waiting to see my nakedness.
For fear of the high-rise
I cover myself.

<sub>Squinting—</sub> <sup>I look up,</sup>


     **silhouettes** seemingly glide
flowing from floor to floor.

                      Slat staring eyes, round eyes


blinds                 between blinds
                    behind blinds

watching the moon's ballet—rising
      and lowering                      freely.


         I open myself wide
                  W I D E
W I D E           for
            the coming of dawn.

## DAWN BRATHWAITE

Hosay: *Last Day*

Coolie Block: the village is empty of chattering neighbours

and boisterous children.

Gone—

like the brown waters in the East Dry River in May.

Streets lined with cracked pavements where

peeping crabgrass tracks the noon

scorching effortlessly.                    Tree leaves still—

except the      buzz buz zing      of      bluebottles.

In the distance, tassa sounds echo against *tadjahs*.      **Ꮂosay!**

Two half-moons dance with men. There! The lone star.

Embers sit quietly in canals while men dance and flaunt
showy frills of green and red. Crescents kiss in a twinkling— then
                    p  a  r  t
                like some lovers do.

## DAWN BRATHWAITE

### ah really want

to tell all yuh some ting buh a doh know how to say it. 'Cause ah want to tell yuh how ah miss meh mother tongue—by using meh mother tongue. Buh ah out here in foreign so long—long, long. And then ah does want to say some ting sweet sweet (as dey does say). To give yuh a sweet joke, buh ah does cyar[1] say it, 'cause ah los dat sweetness meh self. Every ting soun so foreign. Yuh cyar talk to yuh fellowman using yuh mother tongue here in your new-found land. They might say, *"yuh tryin' to sound Trini."* I am TRINI! Buh ah lef so long. Is like writing ah essay and yuh ha to cross your Ts, and DOT yuh EYES to get a GOOD mark. We lowered the Union Jack. We have we own flag now! When we in de school yard, we does talk with we friends one way, buh when we in de classroom, we speak the way we do at home. If we don't, *OUR* parents will tell us, *"Dais how dey does teach all yuh to talk in school? You BET TER talk properly."*

A fissiparous speaking. So it's difficult to tell you how I feel leaving my homeland, to live in another country—that is home, and another country that is home too. Then just so, outta de blue: I experience *dépaysement.*

---

[1] can't

*Kalpana*

A calm prevailed as the horizon stretched out endlessly; the sky and sea blended as they shared the same bright blue. The *S.S. Rani*, Queen of the Sea, glided forward with her three white sails fluttering. Her wooden hull still had the shine of a new vessel. Her flag, a gold lion on a navy-blue background, fluttered back and forth. The berth deck underneath was well-maintained and the hammocks of the crew were close together, giving it a cosy appearance.

A strong wind blew *Rani* towards her destination – Kalpana, the land of lost treasures. Captain Akhil stood at the helm, a solemn expression on his face. The tattered map taped to the table next to him was the only one of its kind. Filled with curious symbols, it pointed out the dangers they would face on their quest. Many had set out on the journey before them without the map, and none had returned.

'Cap'n?' First-mate Kunal appeared at Akhil's side. 'There's a storm approaching. It wasn't there a moment ago but the clouds are quickly gathering.'

He nervously handed over the telescope to his captain.

Akhil knew as he stepped starboard, levelling the telescope towards the horizon, that Kunal would take over the helm deftly. After all these years, some orders could be left unsaid.

He watched as the thunderclouds gathered with mysterious velocity. Akhil checked the direction and speed of the wind and looked at his compass. The needle was spinning around rapidly.

*I have never seen clouds like these before. They aren't moving with the wind...*

A strong gust blew the ship backwards. The crew on deck jolted from the sudden impact. Captain Akhil quickly regained his balance, pressed his captain's hat firmly back into place and took charge. 'All hands on deck! Lower the sails! Secure the ropes!'

His men moved swiftly with the discipline of ants, each aware of their role on the ship. *S.S. Rani* had only been their home for the past two months but the crew had known each other and worked together over many years. Their previous ship, *S.S. Veera*, had been hit by a terrible storm and, thanks to Captain Akhil's leadership, the crew had survived. *Veera*, however, hadn't. It was a sore topic among the crew and they avoided talking about it.

They had used all the money they had salvaged from the sinking ship and bought the Queen of the Sea. She was a beauty. Much smaller than *Veera*, but more magnificent. And *Rani* would deliver them to the lost treasures of Kalpana.

The men worked with all their might as the storm descended on them. Waves raised the ship high and crashed it down like a rollercoaster. The boards groaned but resisted the water's attempts to breach.

'I won't let another storm take my ship,' Akhil muttered to himself. With renewed determination, he began barking out instructions to his crew.

Darkness and cold winds engulfed them. The only light that illuminated their plight came from the ferocious lightning that was trying to split the skies apart. Salt stung their eyes and filled their mouths with the taste of raw fish. Their drenched clothes clung to their bodies. Rain and sea unleashed their fury, rattling the *Rani* and all those who called her home.

'This storm is worse than the last one!' Pranav yelled as he held on to the ropes for dear life.

'Don't mention that storm! No one wants to remember that ...' Sathya said nervously, watching Captain Akhil secure the main sail, and ducking as the boom swung by.

'Don't worry, boys. Cap'n has saved us countless times. He's not going to let you down today!' Kunal called out from the helm.

After what felt like forever, the storm seemed to settle down. The sea stopped its thrashing. Just as the boys began to breathe easy, a loud roar reverberated through the *Rani*, all the way to their very bones.

'What was that?' Pranav asked. Goosebumps prickled every inch of his skin.

'Thunder, maybe?' Sathya squeaked.

'Thunder doesn't come from underwater,' Captain Akhil said, doubt clouding his brow. His hand instinctively inched towards the sword and revolver he kept on his belt.

A silence fell on the ship once again. The uninterrupted raindrops on their skin and the crew's panting were the only noises reminding them that they were not frozen in time.

'Maybe we imagined it?' Sathya said hopefully.

'Oh, yes. *All of us* imagined it.' Kunal's sarcasm cut deep.

'Whatever it was, maybe it's gone now,' Pranav said, infected by Sathya's hopefulness.

Captain Akhil shook his head as he approached his map. He traced the path they had taken and his finger landed on the symbol of a skull. The last obstacle before they would reach Kalpana.

Cautiously, Akhil walked to the bow of the ship. With a leg on the large metal chains of the anchor, he looked over at the suspiciously calm, ink-blue water.

*Sudden storms, underwater roars, A SKULL? Is this why ships have been disappearing?*

A bubble rose to the surface of the water.

*Are we even sure if there is a land called Kalpana? Have I led my men into a trap?*

The bubble burst.

A roar, louder than the previous one, tore through the sea and sky. Captain Akhil watched in horror as a gigantic, yellow head covered in moss and seaweed rose from the surface. Its sharp teeth threatened to snap the ship in two. Its blazing eyes locked with Akhil's and it lunged –

'Akhil!' his mother yelled. 'How long will you sit in the bathtub and splash around?'

'Ma, five more minutes!' Akhil said, annoyed.

'What five more minutes? The water has gone completely cold. If you stay any longer, you'll fall sick. Now turn off the hand shower and get out of the tub.'

Akhil's mom picked him up and set him down on the bathroom mat. She grabbed a towel and wrapped him up.

'You and your *kalpana*,' his mom muttered as she dried his hair. 'Dreaming for hours and hours. You play in the water, play with your friends in Kunal's house, and watch all those nonsense movies with your father. When will you study, huh? And stop splashing in the tub. Look, all the water is on the floor.'

'Okay, Ma.'

'You splashed around and broke your first toy ship. You want to break the new one also or what? I'm going to let you play only with that rubber duck from now on.'

'What will I do with only the monster?' Akhil muttered.

'Monster? What monster?'

'Never mind, Ma.'

*Mum's Secret*

Mummichog was the only person in the room when Grandma died.

When they found out she was gonna bite the dust soon, they set her up in bed with plenty of books on the table, the window open and a glass of whiskey in arm's reach. During that time, the family slept over at Grandma's house, bringing her the newspaper and hardly leaving her side. But it just so happened that everyone left the room for the bathroom, a drink, or some fresh air, when Mum stepped in all by himself. He was a charming boy, and kind. He had graduated high school that year. But whatever Grandma told him that day changed Mummichog.

The story goes that Grandma's children filed back into the room after experiencing a strange feeling. As soon as they realized that she was dead, and saw that Mummichog was shaking in her leaving clutches, they scrambled over her body to say goodbye. Mum's mother asked if Grandma said anything—what were the famous final words?

But Mummichog was silent. He did not speak or mumble or laugh. Whatever he heard in that room with the fresh open window, the hot air of the swamp pulled into the yellowed bedsheets, the glass of whiskey only sampled, sentenced him to a life muted. One where he would never tell this secret, much less talk at all. When Grandma transferred that word, sentence, speech, whatever it was, Mum was transformed.

The middle brother, Minnow, was the first to try to coax the words out of him. He suggested that giving Mummichog the opportunity to write in a diary might eventually draw out his deepest thoughts. While he did write most every day, this plan did not succeed (their mother read his entries and reported that they were ordinary). Each of Grandma's children tried, as well, to no avail. Uncle Vince tried hypnotism (which only made Mum fall asleep). Aunt Bobbie wanted nothing to do with Mummichog (she was the angriest about not being there when Grandma died, and pointed out that Mum would probably outlive Grandma's children—it was unfair that they may never know what their mother said). And it was Aunt Kim who suggested that perhaps Grandma didn't say anything—it was just that Mummichog was not prepared to see someone die.

Someone's cousin was a therapist, and they were asked to come and speak with Mummichog—or better, to get Mummichog to speak. It's safe to say that this was an even worse idea than hypnotism because Mum simply would not cooperate, and walked out in the middle of sessions. Defeated, the therapist suggested taking him to a hospital. Perhaps there was serious trauma that needed medical attention. Was there a far more severe impact left on Mummichog the day Grandma died? Something that haunted him? What if he needed help, and he just couldn't say so? What if he would be silent forever?

But Mum's mother announced that she wouldn't take him anywhere because there was nothing wrong with him. She loved him whether he spoke or not. And as for his mental state, he seemed perfectly content. He did not share the frustrations around him, were they present. Instead of being with his friends, he became reclusive. While once he may have been a chanting, laughing force of passion, he was now something like a little light that was still and serene. Either exceptionally preoccupied or empty. Years passed and the *what* became less interesting; it was the *why* Mum kept to himself. People stopped asking him, and instead asked themselves.

It was the day after Mum's wedding, and the new couple were coming over for lunch. Craw, the youngest brother by quite a few years, was hiding in the parlor, crouched against the door separating him from the kitchen. He hid in neighboring spaces, in closets, under tables, listening to people talk, their footfalls, and waiting for the moment when someone might say, "Where's Craw?" The wedding was no different. He was one of the groomsmen but was nowhere to be found during the ceremony. He wanted to close his eyes and listen to the whole thing from within the warm confines of the chapel coatroom. He would have looked very small standing next to the other men in suits anyway.

Afterward, he was reprimanded for not being there. "But I *was* there," Craw said. "I heard the whole thing." Apparently that wasn't enough.

"It's not a good habit, and you know that already," Mother had said last night. "Missing your brother's wedding—I think Mum was upset." She had gone on to explain what couldn't be heard, what Craw missed— that instead of saying any vows, Mum put his cheek over Polly's ear. When he did, she smiled. Everyone thought that it was very sweet, but it also reignited questions about Mummichog. After all, there were some relatives of Polly's who met him only yesterday, and wondered what was wrong with him.

Craw knew the story, but not well. He had heard it told through many different walls, by many people, and even seen it acted out. But Craw was too young when Grandma died—he couldn't remember a time when Mummichog spoke. To him, his brother had always been like that.

In the parlor, Craw heard Mother let them in. He heard her *Oh*'s when she must have been hugging them, and a loud smooch. Chairs scraped across the floor, the sound of Father and Minnow getting to their feet. Mother was beginning to say that they were making sandwiches when Polly interrupted to say thank you for everything. This prompted muffled weeping, the soft crunch of clothes, another hug.

"I didn't do anything," Mother said. "I'm just so happy for you." Some nose blowing was followed by: "Oh, these are for us? Thank you." Craw heard everyone crowd into the kitchen, their voices becoming a little cleaner, their movements more audible.

"Come in here and tell us what you want," Father said. The sound of plates clinking together, a knife grazing the counter, someone rinsing their hands in the sink. "And then we can get you situated, Mum. How's that?"

Craw migrated from the parlor to the living room, and then to the back porch. It was a screen-protected porch with a plastic table and chairs. He circled the corners of it, examining each spider web individually. He was barefoot, and the rug was rough with tracked-in pine needles and dried storm water. He made his way down the steps, fitting himself between the trees and the foliage that deepened behind the house. The oppressive heat made it difficult to breathe. His toes made imprints on the bloated moss, the soil giving in to him.

Not far off, a rabbit was nibbling among the ferns. Evidently it sensed no danger, as it seemed rather calm. Its angular little head made tremulous movements that meant nothing to Craw, but was perhaps signaling to him something he couldn't understand. As he approached, it turned out of sight. A warbler above him sang a few notes, and then another answered the call. Craw followed the warbler's song, and it led him backwards, back home.

Sitting on the porch was Mummichog, probably waiting for lunch. Craw hadn't seen him since the previous morning, and hadn't thought of how to apologize yet. But he was hearing the warbler still. It was coming from Mum.

Craw scrambled back up the steps and sat beside Mummichog on the porch. "I didn't know you could whistle," he said. He reached out to touch Mummichog's face. He gripped his jaw in his hand. He was shocked to feel sharp stubble, and as he stared into his brother's eyes noticed that he was in fact a man. He was much older than Craw. He had fine lines around his eyes from smiling, freckles on his cheek and nose, perhaps from the sun, and a long and crooked path from the bridge of his nose to his lips, which smirked. Craw wondered if he had ever looked at Mum like that before, really studied him, and decided that he had not. "Do it again."

Mummichog whistled. Craw felt his teeth part, the chin tense up. It was a great, free sound. "Wait, do it again." He let go of Mum and went back inside the house. "Now!"

"What are you doing?" Mother asked from the kitchen.

"*Shhh!*"

"I beg your pardon?"

"I SAID SHHH!" Craw raced to the kitchen and pushed open the window over the sink. He opened all the windows in the dining room, too. He burst out the front door and ran with his hands cupping his ears, his eyes closed. He stopped in the middle of the street somewhere. He could still hear Mum whistling. It was all forgiven.

## ALEX PENLAND

*Ordinary Death*

Welcome, and do not be afraid.

You have died an ordinary death under extraordinary circumstances. We at the Unfulfilled Promises Research Trust understand your alarm at the situation and are working to ensure your transition is as painless as possible. Do not be afraid. Your memories are not gone, but have been temporarily suspended for your comfort.

The Unfulfilled Promises Research Trust is, to you, an extraterrestrial organization. We are dedicated to the preservation and memorialization of cultures which have been lost before they were able to fulfill their true potential. Our organization identifies fledgling species that are deemed at risk for untimely extermination—often due to self-destructive tendencies, perilous evolutionary circumstances, or impending conquest—and gathers as much information on them as is realistically possible to preserve. With this information we create and maintain a list of potential subjects for trial should the necessity arise. In the event of a fledgling species' demise, these potential subjects are then screened and a small number are selected for resurrection.

We regret to inform you that this is what has happened to the human species. You are one of twelve representatives of your planet chosen for trial, and one of six human beings.

You will undoubtedly have questions. Many of them cannot be answered yet. Those which *can* be answered, I will answer now.

•

## Why has access to my personal memory been suspended?

Past experience has shown that immediate access to personal memories—such as the faces of loved ones or the circumstances of one's death—cause more distress than comfort. These memories will be released to you throughout the trial. Impersonal knowledge, such as arithmetic, cultural history and media, and the name of your species, should still be accessible.

If you find yourself unable to access impersonal knowledge, please report to me for immediate termination.

## Will the other member(s) of my species be someone I know?

The estimated chance of your being connected to the other human beings undergoing trial is roughly five in seven billion. While not impossible, it is extremely unlikely that you will have crossed paths. Additionally, you will not be introduced to one another until after the first examinations of the trial have been completed, so it is best not to dwell on their existence.

## Is it possible to bring back someone I love?

No. The Trust has extremely limited resources. We apologize for this inconvenience.

## What happened to my planet?

Earth itself is still present, but the majority of life has been extinguished. According to our research you should already be aware of the major contributor, which is common knowledge rather than memory: a small group of influential human beings created systematic changes to the atmosphere, which caused irreparable changes in your natural environment. For various reasons your species was unable to fight these changes in meaningful ways. This was the catalyst for fires, floods, and damaging storms, as well as damage to infrastructure. The ensuing political friction caused war, which ended the lives of anyone who had survived the initial turbulence.

•

Other questions will be answered in person. Your memories will be released to you as the trial progresses. In the meantime, this is what you can expect:

The trial will last for a period of 216 days ("days" here are defined by your home planet's rotation) in which your suitability will be assessed. During that time you will complete a number of projects and undergo a series of examinations, both physical and mental. The outcome of these examinations will determine your species' potential for growth and readiness for the galactic stage. If you are successful in your examinations, a petition will be submitted on your behalf, which if accepted will register your species in the intergalactic community. An acceptance will also allow the Unfulfilled Promises Research Trust to allocate its resources to your continued survival. We regret that we do not have enough resources to continue to provide for species which are not successful in their petition.

My name is multitudes, but for simplicity's sake you may call me Eve. I will be your case manager for the next 216 days and will guide you through the trial. I will be in touch—in person—very soon.

When we meet, your trial will begin. Good luck.

# HAYLEY BERNIER

*You're sorry and*

you're not afraid of my feelings, you say
as you pull the door closed behind you.
I peer through mirrors, at wavering handles,
hoping every corner or threshold
will have you hidden in a hue.

As if there is some match
to be lit or blown or won—
you throw it into the water
with placid feathers you've plucked
from our inside joke that has spun undone.

There are stories I don't know
how to pry from my heath;
explanations over excuses
I fall short, fall forward, throwing myself
at your feet but not beneath.

I thought these were breaches
I'd forgiven and swallowed—
Denial is our most affable friend.
Just a joke inside a familiar body—
Ardour and Obsession, I don't want to be followed.

Exorcise me, I am ready now,
after years and days of yearning.
Scrape the tenderness from my hands
and peel me from Devotion;
there are letters I should be burning.

## HAYLEY BERNIER

*Aghast*

I finally feel you; I'd thought you'd gone.
A chill in every finger, here, goosebumps
raised in awe of you, do you still push on?
Finally back at the door your fist thumps,

hallucinating heart sliding down my back—
why did you leave if you are here again?
Crude wit cursed resident insomniac:
crouch beside the record player now, then

play your lost music, skin fire, lacking air
empty doorway—is this you here        I know
you wanted versed clean breeze, it isn't fair
more stitches into years I try to sew.

Choking chin, tooth grin, this is you I feel;
foreign trauma body: beg me unreal.

## HAYLEY BERNIER

*Since You Left the Earth I Have Forgotten How to Cry Out About Anything Else*

you are charcoal
call me black-handed
etching your ideas down
my fingers dance as
fast as
the ink can run
I bet on a winning splash-dark
the speckling will look like
the age spots on your
yellow tobacco
middle finger
give me your patchouli blood
give me your leather feet
give me your hound dog singing heart
throb on every wall
give me your laughing voice
so that I may speak again

what beautiful curls of brain matter
the tangled highways
with too many exits and junctions
the streetlights off
now just one dusty country road
all the branches full leaf
the powdered air settles
slowly into green fields
every direction we look
just grass and trees
some horses
they look at me with your eyes
and I wonder who is driving
but it doesn't matter anymore
because there is only one way to go
and we are going

*The Good Night*

"No... I'm not religious," I replied. As the winter sun was setting early and there was not enough light, the old man closed a small book of sutras in vertical form, flattened each corner, and placed it in an inner pocket of his coat, which had been sewn close to his chest. Then, as if taking a rest, he took out his thermos, blew away the rising mist, looked straight ahead and sipped his tea carefully.

I was finally interested in the old man and his topic, since we were sitting on a wobbling bus for such a long time and he was as comfortable as if he were at a teahouse. He was holding his book before I struggled to sit there, and barely changed his gesture: bowed his back to recognize every word, one hand to hold the book and one hand to point at the lines. He was so concentrated that I was surprised he would even start a conversation.

"Faith gives me peace," he said, looking up at me. "I'm on my way to a weekly lecture at the Buddhist Center. Some teachers there are highly respected monks, some teachers are university lecturers. We attach great importance to the cultural interpretation of Buddhist scriptures, not blind worship."

His voice was calm and firm, but I had to work hard to suppress my laughter. Because the bus was filling up and the temperature was rising, his glasses were steamy with tea while he talked about such serious subjects. His eyes and the wrinkles around the corners of them, magnified by his reading glasses, made him look like a strange old man from a comic book.

"Aside from the peace, what makes you so convinced that what you believe is true?" I looked out the window and enjoyed the view. As dusk settled and artificial light began to take over the city, students were leaving school and workers were heading home. Good. I always felt safer in the crowd because fewer people would notice me. I had to try to ignore the tingling sensation in my legs, where the skin was harder after it had grown back from the burns. It was probably too hot in that crowded bus.

The humid air did not affect him in the least, and he still spoke to me in a calm tone. "Young man, why don't I tell you a story?"

A sudden brake interrupted him, and we involuntarily put our hands on the seat in front of us. Someone sitting in front looked back for a moment, and then asked with concern if I was all right. I knew she meant well, but I just nodded with my eyes dodging hers.

He saw my reaction to the girl and went on, "I know a monk..." Another abrupt brake. An old man with a white beard and a tall boy came in from the front door. The boy's head almost touched the bus roof.

"He is in a temple in the suburb, regardless of wind, frost, rain and snow, wearing ordinary monk clothing and sweeping the floor every day. In autumn..." This religious old man continued. The girl in front of me offered her seat to the white beard. The white beard said thank you and turned his head to the boy who followed him. "Come and sit!" he said. I could clearly feel that the eyes of others in this narrow bus were expressing their doubts towards them. The boy, like the center of a doubt whirlpool, stumbled towards me. Then I was at the center of it, too. I lifted my hand to wipe the sweat from my forehead. I forced myself back into the religious man's story, trying to shake the embarrassment and the prickling feeling off.

"... He sweeps leaves to the roots of the trees in the morning mist, clasps his hands and says, *Go to where you belong...*"

*Are we sweepers? Or are we falling leaves, rolling on the ground back to where we belong?* I thought.

The bus continued to move forward, endlessly. When the passenger who was about to get off stood up, the white beard seized the opportunity to have a seat in front of his grandson, leaving the other passengers without seats to stand. It left the boy, the white beard and me; the three of us joined together to form a line like a dam, collecting doubts from all directions.

"... The autumn wind will come, but he does not care. Just sweeps the slate road again when someone comes..."

The boy kept shaking his body in his own rhythm, in addition to the bus. His eyes kept moving from the window and back to his grandfather, as if he was afraid that in the next second, his grandfather would be gone. I could see clearly the blood vessel near the boy's temple, a worm-like twist.

Poor worm.

The religious old man seemed to sense my mind wandering. It wasn't until I looked down at him again that he said slowly, "This is what he does every day, every day. Believing in your choices is a tribulation for everyone." He stared at my feet. "You don't seem to have cultivated your heart, young man."

The old man's needle-like eyesight pinned me to the seat. Panic and pain sealed my mouth like a piece of tape, and for a long time I could make no sound. My legs even started to cramp, so I put my things down and pressed my thighs with both hands. My fingers nearly wedged into the flesh. I flicked my eyes straight ahead and saw that the boy was as bewildered as I was. He was wearing two hooded pullovers, and the hoods were tangled. Then there was his grandfather's straight back, and the back of his head that never changed direction, with neat gray stubble... The hot smell of human beings in the bus steamed my ears red.

The bus stopped again. Through the misty window, I saw the ancient temple hidden among the branches on the hill. I realized that we had arrived at the Temple Station. Many people were coming out of the temple and walking down the long steps. The old man was going to get off here. He handed me the card of the Buddhist Center. "Come to us at any time, if you need spiritual help, whether you believe in religion or not... or physical training. Look, there are stairs that lead up to the temple." He chuckled and got out of the bus, with a hand on his chest as he walked through the crowd.

And the boy in front of me, holding his grandfather's seat back, suddenly became fretful. He kept getting up and sitting down awkwardly, "Grandpa, Grandpa!" He was so anxious that he could only pronounce such syllables.

The white beard slowly got up and gave a cold order: "Get out of the bus." They walked down the middle of the bus. Like when they had got on, the white beard still treated his grandson coldly, leaving only the back of his head for his grandson to chase unsteadily. But I believe that the white beard had slowed down his pace.

Holding the small white card in my hand, I read the gold letters on it. *The Tathagata, came from nowhere, went to nowhere, hence the name is Tathagata.* I searched every corner of the words with my eyes, and at last I had the strength to pick up my things. Pick up... Oh, yes, a pair of crutches. My crutches.

After the gas explosion, it seemed as though I got used to my crutches. At first, I lost my left leg. Three skin grafts were performed within five months of hospitalization. All things during that period of time passed like a nightmare, leaving only painful memories. Now, I always go to the hospital at night to be prescribed anti-inflammatory drugs, as under the darkness I know people won't recognize me.

Seeing me picking up my crutches, the girl sitting in front of me helped me to stand up and said, "Are you getting off?"

This time I was not as embarrassed as a balloon about to explode, and said, "Yes, next stop. Thank you... thank you." She had a beautiful mole at the corner of her eye, and her eyes curved like two pairs of rainbows when she smiled. Her eyes sparkled like a lake in the moonlight. Oh, the moonlight I knew in the old days.

Yes, I was going to get off the bus, and walk into the crowd. Walk into the good night with the religious old man, the painful grandfather, the tall slow-witted boy, the students chasing each other, and all the people going home.

## ERIN LYONS

*The Christmas Tree*

At Christmas time people are unreasonably cheery. Bundled up in scarves and mitts, they sing along to overplayed Christmas songs, drink hot chocolate/mulled wine/all alcohol with wild abandon and smile until their faces hurt. Each person seems to have a glittery glow about them, as though they are made of tinsel, as though they might just burst open and spray holiday confetti all around. It's as if the whole world is shouting: *Be happy, merry, and bright!* But all Neetu wants to do is tell them to piss off and bury her head under pillows and not wake up till spring.

Last Christmas they got a tree.

For the first time in forty-one years of marriage, an actual Christmas tree. Usually, they just strung a few lights from the fig plant that sat in their front window – the same lights Neetu put up for Diwali. Neetu had only begun celebrating Christmas after she'd married Richard; before that, Christmas was just something else she observed other people doing that her family did not.

Richard and Neetu hadn't gotten a Christmas tree before because Richard had said it was too much of a hassle to put up and take down again two weeks later. But suddenly Richard said he wanted a great big tree.

'How will we get it home?' she said.

'I'll carry it,' he said.

Richard and Neetu were sitting in the kitchen having breakfast. The room smelt of coffee, cardamom, and cinnamon. Morning light filtered in through the tall window and spread across the table where they sat. Outside, a tall chestnut tree strangled in vines was being battered by the wind; the few leaves that had clung on until December finally gave up and blew away.

Neetu rolled her eyes. '*You'll* carry it?' she said.

'Yes, why not?'

'Because you're sixty-three, not twenty-three.'

'Fine, we'll take the bus.'

'I don't know why you suddenly want a Christmas tree.'

'I'm feeling festive.' And here Richard filled up his lungs and thumped his chest with both fists.

Neetu couldn't help but laugh, causing a dimple to sprout on her left cheek. Then she said, very seriously, 'You can't take a tree on a bus.'

'Why not?' said Richard, looking slightly hurt, with a mouth full of porridge.

'It won't fit.'

Richard washed the porridge down with his coffee. 'It would,' he said.

'We would get needles all over the bus, and what if someone has an allergy?'

'An allergy? To Christmas trees?'

'Yes.'

'Fine, *we'll* walk it home.'

'It's nearly a mile away, *and* a hill.'

'*Down* a hill.' He grinned.


Neetu is sitting on the sofa with her feet up and a newspaper in her hand. There is a cup of hot tea sitting on the coffee table beside her. Earl Grey. Its steam is misting the air. But Neetu is not reading the newspaper; she is staring at the space in the bay window where the Christmas tree stood last year. Now it is just the lightless fig plant and the armchair.

Last night carollers turned up. The doorbell rang, and when she swung open the door there they were, eight little bodies huddled together like stuffed sausages in thick winter coats, wearing blinking red noses and reindeer antlers on their heads. Their parents beamed proudly behind them, smiling so much – too much – that Neetu nearly smiled back.

Then the children began to sing 'Silent Night' and Neetu had to close the door.

The sound of 'Silent Night' had floated out of the church as Richard and Neetu struggled past it, dragging their eight-foot Christmas tree. Although it was early afternoon, the air already had the crispness of evening. Neetu's nose was red from the cold and she could see the cloud of her breath as her hand slipped on the damp tree trunk.

'Stop,' she said.

'What's wrong?' he said.

'Just put the bloody tree down.'

The Christmas tree landed on the pavement with a thud.

'Why did we get the biggest tree on the lot?' said Neetu, shaking out her wrists.

'There were bigger trees,' Richard protested.

'Well why did they give us this bloody brick at the bottom?'

'It's a free and natural tree stand.' He beamed. The stand was a cut log from a much bigger tree, which weighed the same amount as the Christmas tree itself (or more).

'My back hurts.' Neetu winced.

Richard and Neetu rested on the steps of the church. The sliding doors opened and closed as members went in and out, causing the sound of the choir to come in soft and loud waves.

*All is calm …*

*All is bright …*

From the top of Morningside Road, the less than a mile that remained looked more like ten with the tree. On the pavement, people rushed by with full shopping bags in tow – only two weeks left until Christmas. The Christmas lights attached at the tops of the lamp posts switched on as a little girl, swung by her hands by both parents, let out high-pitched giggles mid-flight. Richard patted Neetu's hand, brushed a strand of black-grey hair from her face and kissed her gently on the cheek. They hadn't been lucky in having children, and still, at sixty-one, sometimes Neetu felt a sadness wash over her when she saw young families.

They sat on the steps until the choir stopped singing.

'Come on, you old fart,' said Neetu, standing up.

Richard and Neetu picked up the tree again, Neetu in the back with the top, and Richard in the front with the heavy bottom. Every ten feet or so they would have to put the tree down and rest, and the fifteen-minute walk home turned into an hour. Passers-by smiled and offered, 'Big tree!' as they squeezed past, in too much of a hurry to lend a hand to the retired couple struggling down the hill with a ridiculous eight-foot tree.

The sky filled with slate grey clouds that rumbled and opened up, soaking Richard and Neetu as they continued, bickering all the way home.


Neetu hasn't put any decorations up this year. She hasn't done any Christmas baking – no shortbread cookies or mince pies or cinnamon ginger loaves that she used to pride herself on to please Richard.

She has hardly left the house.

The roads are icy, and she has had a bad back ever since they dragged that bloody Christmas tree home last year. She is worried she will slip if she goes outside. She has no Richard to hold her hand. And no Richard to look over at and laugh with when she does slip.


Richard put his hand on Neetu's and clasped her fingers. He had several long cuts on his hands from handling the tree, and Neetu's back ached. They sat snuggled on the sofa, admiring the result of their work.

Their short string of lights only wrapped round the top portion of the Christmas tree – making the bottom half appear dark and forgotten. Outside the night was black, and the lights reflected like soft candles in the window. The smell of wet pine hung in the air.

'Worth it?' he said, his breath smelling of the dram they shared.

'Absolutely fucking worth it,' she said.


Neetu gets up. She has decided to take a walk. To get some fresh air, get out of the house, and brave the merriness that lies in wait. In the front hall she takes her scarf from the hanger, then bundles up in her coat, doing her buttons all the way up to the top.

She pauses when she opens the front door, looks back at the coat rack on the wall, sure she's forgotten something. Then she catches sight of Richard's grey knitted sweater hanging up, hidden behind an umbrella. She must have missed it when she was gathering up his things.

She stops. Everything stops.

She removes the umbrella and sets it down in the corner. Carefully, she takes the sweater off the hook, afraid it will unravel and fall apart.

Him.

It's him.

She brings the sweater to her nose and breathes him in, hiding her face in the bristly wool, trying to smell in the deepest possible way – to smell with extra senses – as if she will crumble if she misses one microscopic trail of a scent.

It is not a smell to be described, only to be identified with the image of Richard, her Richard, warm-bodied Richard with happy crow's feet lines in the corners of his eyes, Richard with his soft reddish beard – Neetu's nesting ground – Richard who was always wrapping his arms round her and pinching her bum.

Neetu closes the front door, still inside, in her coat, scarf, and boots, walks down the hall to the bedroom, lifts the duvet, crawls back into bed with the sweater, and does not leave for the rest of the day.

DAVID BLAKESLEE

*Collision*

Right now, the boy with the little red bike (the one with the slipping chain
that his father had promised to fix but never did) is hurtling down the
hill at the end of the cul-de-sac on 88th Place Southwest. The neighbor
girl, with her bowl-cut blond hair (which she had begged her mother for
and then immediately despised) and her white hand-me-down Nikes, is
pedaling hard along 88th Place toward the cul-de-sac where both children
live.

He is passing the orange house that has ten cars in the driveway (which
is home to a man with a full meth lab in his garage). She is rapidly biking
by the woman who lives in the ditch next to the stop sign on the corner of
88th and Holly Drive.

In 25 seconds, the boy will reach the end of the hill, and the girl will
turn left into the cul-de-sac. When the bikes collide, the girl will be mostly
fine, and the boy will flip over his handlebars and break his front tooth in
half on the pavement.

In 50 seconds, he will run home, and his mother will call the dentist
even though she doesn't know where she will get the money to fix his tooth
because her husband is out of a job and she was in the hospital all winter
long due to complications of the birth of the boy's little brother.

In 10 minutes, the girl will watch from the sidewalk as the boy gets into
the beaten-up family minivan and is driven away (she won't know what
to say).

In two hours, the boy will be wriggling uncomfortably in a dentist's
chair, with blood dried on the corner of his mouth because his bottom
lip has split open too (but the dentist can't really do anything about that).

In three days, the boy will ride his bike again and the neighbor girl will
say sorry and show him her scraped knee.

In two weeks, they will learn that they are in the same class in school in the upcoming year and that they both like reading mysteries.

In one month, they will hold hands in the dark during the "red" lockdown when the man with the gun who has just robbed the convenience store tries to hide behind one of the buildings on campus. They will stifle their screams when they see silhouettes cross the window shades and hear the sirens and the police with their megaphones.

In three years, the girl's mother will die unexpectedly.

In three years and four days, the boy will see the girl kicking at rocks outside school (he won't know what to say).

In four years, she will move away with her aunt and uncle and go to a different school somewhere in California. He will never see her again.


But right now, before the collision, the girl is shaking her head as the wind whips through her hair. The boy is lifting his feet off the pedals and letting his shirt flap behind him like a cape. And they are both closing their eyes because it's a late afternoon in the summer, and they both like riding their bikes really fast.

## SPECIAL THANKS

...from all involved to everybody who supported us personally, and to:

Tracey S. Rosenberg, Edinburgh University writer in residence, for advice, support, and organising helpful events.

Jane McKie, Creative Writing MSc programme director, for advice, support, and extraordinarily competent and kind leadership through difficult times.

Jane Alexander, Robert Alan Jamieson, Patrick James Errington, Alan Gillis, Allyson Stack, Alice Thompson, and Miriam Gamble, creative writing professors, for their invaluable support, feedback, advice, encouragement, and kindness.

James T. Harding, for friendly and expert publishing advice.

Ann Landmann, for friendly and expert publishing and event-management advice.

Magali Román, Merel De Beer, and Sonali Misra, for passing on their expertise from FAS in previous years.

Lighthouse Books, for creating community in the face of chaos and for kind support and expert advice.

Blackwell's, for planning a launch party with us that will hopefully happen at some point.

Ella Keam, for quick, consistent, and friendly support.

Kara McCormack, for keeping us sane during exam time.

Last but not least to the department of Languages, Literatures and Cultures at the University of Edinburgh for creating this opportunity.

# CONTRIBUTORS

HAYLEY BERNIER is doing her MSc in creative writing here in Edinburgh, with a focus in poetry. She holds a bachelor's degree in English literature with a creative writing minor, having graduated with honours from Bishop's University in Quebec, Canada. Hayley's work appears in the 2017 edition of *The Mitre*, her alma mater's yearly publication. She loves animals, rain, vegetarian snacks, and train rides through the Highlands. Hayley's long-term goals are to publish her works of writing, hopefully in a variety of genres (poetry, short fiction, novels, non-fiction) à la Margaret Atwood.

DAVID BLAKESLEE grew up in some suburb in the Pacific Northwest. He is a well-adjusted loner who spends a lot of time in the library. Once in a blue moon, if the mood is right, he sits down to write something.

DAWN BRATHWAITE was born in the Republic of Trinidad and Tobago and calls two other countries home. In her poem 'ah really want', she reflects on her status as a multi-citizen. While an undergraduate at the University of Richmond, USA, Dawn was awarded the George O. Squires Scholarship in Creative Writing for her work in poetry. She also writes short stories. Dawn has played the steel pan (tenor) competitively, is an avid photographer, and has exhibited her work in the United States. She is currently completing a MSc in creative writing at the University of Edinburgh.

RUTH BROWN is a writer from South London. She specialises in nothing and everything.

THOMAS CARROLL is a fiction writer interested in exploring the questions posed against humanity, both in everyday life and in the dystopian and science-fiction realities which he often creates. After completing his master's degree at the University of Edinburgh, he hopes to explore writing in various creative industries.

BRUNA CASTELO BRANCO is a Brazilian journalist. She worked at a weekly magazine in Brazil and used to write about literature for a children's newspaper. As part of her final undergraduate project, she wrote a novella about her great-grandmother's life based on her grandmother's childhood memories. Although she doesn't have a good memory, she loves exploring archives and all kinds of memorabilia.

ALEXA CASTILLO was born in Texas and graduated from the University of St Andrews with an MA in English literature prior to the commencement of the MSc in creative writing. She is inspired by the works of William Faulkner and Haruki Murakami and the short stories of Roald Dahl. Specifically, the complexity of memory, emotion, and temporality are aspects that she integrates into her work, aiming to capture a paradoxically surreal verisimilitude.

ANTHI CHEIMARIOU holds a BA in English and American literature from the American College of Greece. She is currently pursuing an MSc in creative writing at the University of Edinburgh. She was long-listed in the Poetry Society's National Poetry Competition in 2017 with her poem 'Leftovers'. Identifying herself as a poet, Anthi was also classically trained in piano and cello from a young age, having received numerous distinctions until the age of 16, and hopes that her love of music and by extension of mathematics will manifest in her poetry.

EMERSON ROSE CRAIG is a writer from Portland, Oregon, USA. She worked as an editorial intern for CALYX Press before moving to Edinburgh. She specialises in writing fantastical and surreal fiction for children and young adults. Her work has previously been published by WritersWeekly.com.

NIKOLA DIMITROV is a high-functioning daydreamer who spends his time writing *Love Letters to the Universe*, a collection of science fiction short stories. His first published work, 'Calliope's Laughter', appears in the online journal *Tint*. In 2018 he graduated from Goethe Universität after completing a mind-melting thesis on the relationship between religion and science in the Golden Age of sci-fi, which he enjoys reading to his grandmother. For most of his life, he has been exploring different countries, languages, and cultures and he plans to keep enriching and expanding his worldview for the benefit of his writing.

WREN T. FLEMING writes long fiction and sometimes short fiction. She is from Des Moines, Iowa, and is a graduate of the University of Iowa. She's published in the student-organised literary review called *Earthwords*. She's also a connoisseur of French toast.

LOLA GAZTAÑAGA BAGGEN is a multinational anti-nationalist polyglot with a penchant for black clothes, colourful scarves, and anything folklore. Having lived in the wonderfully gothic Edinburgh for almost three years now, she takes full inspiration to write the dark, magical, and disturbed. However, a childhood spent in Holland and Spain means she also specialises in dyke reviews and siesta manuals.

BHAVIKA GOVIL is a fiction writer from India who loves writing about people, and the strange and wonderful things they feel and do. Before pursuing a master's in creative writing at the University of Edinburgh, she worked in publishing and media as a features writer. Her work has been featured in places like *Vogue* India, *Outlook Traveller*, *The Lookout Journal*, and *Little Black Book* and she is the winner of the Bound Short Story Contest 2019. Say hi to her at bhavikagovil@gmail.com. She's not bad at writing (back).

BETH GRAINGER is a poet from the North of England who endeavours to write powerful and empathetic verse centring around those on the margins and society, social deprivation, and human experience. She graduated from the University of Edinburgh with honours in 2019 and is currently pursuing an MSc in creative writing.

LESLIE GROLLMAN's work appears in *Nailed Magazine*, *Thimble Literary Magazine*, *Pathos Literary Magazine*, *Spark*, *Write Like You're Alive Anthology* 2016 and 2018, and is forthcoming. Her stuff is in storage in Portland, Oregon; her mail goes to her brother in Baltimore. She likes the sounds of shoes clicking cobblestones.

JULIANN GUERRA is a Massachusetts native who enjoys writing in the new adult genre. As an undergraduate, she worked as a writing assistant for other students and was the news editor for the college newspaper. She has a blog called 'Books, Travel, Life, etc.' that she has been updating since she was eighteen. When she's not writing, Juliann enjoys adding books to her shelves and stamps to her passport.

JULIA GUILLERMINA is a Spanish and French writer. She studied humanities, although she has a mathematical mind, and specialised in medieval history. Curious, ambitious, and impatient, she began writing at ten and got used to it in the world of fanfiction. She is passionate about languages and poetry – she is also a musician. She writes short and long fiction, and uses it to understand human relationships. She believes her best defence is humour.

KATIE HAY is a creative writer and Christian artist from Sapelo Island, Georgia (USA). She loves talking, listening, writing, singing, cooking, outdoorsy things, and being a goof. Though her current pursuit of a creative writing MSc demands she spend much time sitting hunched over a computer or notebook, she still finds plenty of time for running around and loudly laughing with friends. She errs on the side of longer fantastic and realistic fiction for kids and young adults, exploring questions of faith and the complexities of being human with other humans. Her website is hay210.com.

MICHAEL HOWRIE grew up in the Lake District, mucking about down all the ginnels and snickets he could find. He went on to study English literature, film, and theatre for his undergrad, constantly fighting against the 'English' in English literature by studying as many languages on the side as his time would allow. Before undertaking his master's, he took a detour via Milan on the way up to Edinburgh and now begrudgingly admits that Italian food is pretty good. He tends to write about nature, almost always with the fantastic in mind, and is most inspired by Diana Wynne Jones.

SAOIRSE IBARGÜEN is a writer and performer from Florida's Gulf Coast. She has spent the past seven years working at the happiest place on earth, while writing bleak and fairly unhappy stories. Saoirse holds a BA in literature from the University of South Florida, and will complete the Creative Writing MSc at the University of Edinburgh in 2020. While she enjoys writing fiction, she spends equal time having adventures and writing memoirs about them. Her most recent work tells the story of her six-month thru-hike of the Appalachian Trail. For Saoirse, writing and exploring go hand in hand.

ZALA JAMBROVIC HATIC is a Slovenian writer and editor currently based in Edinburgh. She holds a double BA in English and French from the University of Ljubljana, though she also attended Université de Nantes and Queen's University Belfast as part of a study exchange programme during her undergraduate studies. She volunteers as a beta reader in her free time. An avid foodie and full-time bookworm, she enjoys discovering new fictional worlds as well as creating her own.

ANNA JONES is a fiction writer from Warwick, England.

JAKE KENDALL writes damp jokes and sad humour. He is interested in tragicomedy, thwarted lives, and themes around disappointment. His short stories have contaminated a number of online journals and websites. He also has an active interest in art history, and has begun writing on the subject. 'A Grave Matter' first appeared in the Cabinet of Heed's February 2020 edition under the title 'An Awful Sight'.

L. K. KRAUS (Lena Kraus) is a writer and translator with ties to Germany, Cornwall, and Norway. She writes realistic fiction, exploring how stories can tell the truth without being the truth. Before moving to Edinburgh, Lena was the chair of the European Democratic Education Community, promoting Democratic Education in Europe and beyond and researching narratives of achievement. She loves mushrooms and will shower her friends in their Latin names unsolicitedly. She is a keen paddler and has completed the longest canoe race in the world twice. Lena is the editor-in-chief of this anthology. Her website is lena-kraus.com.

WENDY LAW was born and grew up in Hong Kong. Many of her works are shadowed by the city's urban landscape, people, and current political unrest. The city is a showcase of how the absurd and the surreal are, in fact, the reality. With the city in her mind, she will continue writing, hoping that one day she will be qualified to call herself a writer.

XUAN LIU comes from China. She loves stories and thinks the meaning of writing is to find 'you'. Indeed, her belief is that stories are full of power and she hopes hers will resonate with readers and make them no longer feel isolated. She is also striving to publish a collection of short stories.

ERIN LYONS is a writer currently working on a collection of short stories and completing an MSc in creative writing. She is interested in the psychology of her characters as they move through moments of love, loss, and loneliness, and the absurdity of those moments. Erin is inspired by the lyricism and playfulness of contemporary Scottish writers. Originally from Canada, she relocated to Spain, where she worked as an English teacher and began studying fiction, before settling in sunny Edinburgh. Aside from these things, Erin likes to lace up her hiking boots and cartwheel over Munros.

HARRISON MACLEOD-BONNAR is a Scottish writer born and raised in Edinburgh. His writing interests include realism, music, time, and Scottish identity. He plans to work on his first novel in 2020.

MARSHEA MAKOSA is a writer and poet with a bachelor's degree in geology; a keen witness to the reckless harmony of the universe. She used to do stand-up for a hot second and then focussed her craft by writing and producing a radioplay, *Of Sapiens and Stars*, and a small angsty chapbook on Etsy titled *Grotesquely Unaffected*. Some of her essays can be found at medium.com/@moushmakosa. She thinks cheese is overrated, and that the African Diaspora is lit. Her Instagram is @gamuchiraiistrue.

M. H. MONICA fell in love with books at the age of three. She's a writer, editor, and animal enthusiast from India. Securing an award in British Council's Agatha Christie Short Story competition propelled her desire to become a writer. When she isn't immersed in a make-believe world of her own creation, she likes to curl up with a good book, movie, or anime. Some of the genres she likes to dabble in are mystery, thriller, fantasy, and sci-fi. Monica will complete her MSc in creative writing at the University of Edinburgh in 2020.

KIT NICHOLSON is a fiction writer and cycling journalist who moved to Edinburgh to pursue creative writing because of Robin Williams. She tends to write about deeply thoughtful characters – troubled artist types – in contemporary and historical settings, and likes to explore the fickleness of memory.

KATHERINE O'CONNELL is a fiction writer from Brooklyn, New York. She completed her undergraduate degree at New York University's Tisch School of the Arts, graduating with honours. When not working on her debut novel, she is overhauling course catalogues for American universities. Her work has been featured in ¡Viva Mercy! magazine.

ANNA O'CONNOR is a writer and visual artist from Portland, Oregon. Her work explores distance and desire in young adulthood, often with touches of the fantastic or surreal. Her poetry has appeared in *Stereoscope Magazine* and *Windowcat*, and her artwork can be viewed at cargocollective.com/annao. She currently lives in Scotland.

ABIGAIL O'NEILL is a prose writer, with a first-class undergraduate degree from the University of Greenwich. Her work has been published in several anthologies and she has had a play performed at the Greenwich Book Festival in 2018. She was also the co-founder and managing editor for *Projector Magazine*. She is enjoying furthering her studies at Edinburgh.

ALEX PENLAND was a museum kid: the Smithsonian museums in Washington, D.C., are the closest thing they have to a hometown. A lifetime in the field around scientists and artists shows itself in their work, which explores themes of agency and interpersonal conflict under adventurous circumstances. You can find more of their work under their pseudonym, Alexandra Penn, at alexandrapenn.com, or follow them @alexpenname on most social media.

ABBIE RANDALL is a writer from Colorado who is currently pursuing an MSc in creative writing at the University of Edinburgh. She previously graduated from the University of Denver with a Bachelor of Arts in creative writing and communications. She enjoys writing fiction with a touch of the fantastical, magical, or eerie. Most of her time is spent in a cafe with a cappuccino and a good book.

OLIVER RAYMOND is a writer from Melbourne, Australia. He wanders the streets in search of weird tableaux and uncanny urbanity. He is turning his attention to putting into words his impressions of art, architecture, and the chaotic beauty that exists when the mundane becomes strange.

ALICE ROGERS did her undergrad in American literature and history at the University of Birmingham, and now spends her days wishing she could reclaim the time that she spent reading Jack Kerouac for class. She likes to write American historical fiction.

TESS SIMPSON is a writer who grew up in the countryside near Oxford. She graduated from Warwick University with a BA in history and can't help writing the past into her fiction. If you have a dog, she would love to meet them.

SHYLA TAPSCOTT is a fiction writer and history enthusiast from Alabama. She holds a BA in history from Columbus State University in Georgia. She enjoys reading, playing video games, and watching movies when she isn't writing – anything to keep her imagination active. She blames the lack of sweet iced tea in Edinburgh for all imminent bouts of ennui that produce her historical horror short stories.

LAUREN N. THURMAN is a writer and editor. Originally from Colorado, she worked in Washington, D.C., as a professional internet user for several years before coming to the University of Edinburgh to pursue a master's in creative writing. She writes about the weird and the lonely, the quiet and the fantastic. Her stories have been featured in *Quaint Magazine* and on *The Moth Radio Hour*. Find more of her work and get in touch at lnthurman.com.

EILEEN VANDERGRIFT is an American poet with Irish roots. Her poems braid the significant vocations that have shaped her: daughter, sister, mother, wife, psychologist, and writer. She lives in Colorado with her husband, Paul. In dog years, she is nine!

CHENSHUO WANG is his Chinese name, and his friends like to call him Chris. He is doing his master's degree in creative writing and is always suffering from nostalgia, though he claims he has never missed his home and past. His works mainly comprise short stories and novellas whose characters and plots are extracted from his personalities and experiences. Although he loves writing and sharing his stories, he is always panicking about his grades and the uncertainty of his future. He wants to be a war correspondent, but he probably won't because he is good at daydreaming.

ZHANGLU WANG is currently a student at the University of Edinburgh. She has an interest in observing human relationships and is at times surprised by how weird and amusing they can be.

SKYE WILSON is a glittery, rugby-playing feminist who spends her time all over Scotland. She studied at Strathclyde before beginning her MSc in creative writing. Skye loves ugly shirts, Oxford commas, and writing poetry about womanhood, hope, and belonging.

TODD WORKMAN, aka Boris, aka Anapachi, is a linguaphile with a penchant for staring at the ocean or the constellations and feeling the vastness of the universe – and stuff. Chocolate chip cookies, climbing trees, and playing with LEGOs are some of his favourite things (for when the dog bites, or when the bee stings). The greatest works he's had the honour to create are his two children.

YUE YANG is an explorer and daydreamer from China. The raindrops like tears falling from the eaves, the yawns of the cat in the sun, the pepper grains like boats in the porridge, the blade of the murderer's blood dripping, the moon with purple halo, the smell of harmful chemicals in the factory, the wild animals dead in the fire, the howl and desire in mythology are all her stories. It's too tiring to chase the stars. Come and count the stars with her instead, no matter where you are, in any form – novels, comics, music, dance.

ALEXANDRA YE is a fiction writer from Great Mills, Maryland.